PROFESSOR LAW

JONATHAN D. ROSEN
AMIN NASSER

1

THE ALLIGATORS MOVED IN FROM ALL DIRECTIONS, SMELLING blood in the murky water. More alligators started to circle the small boat rocking in the water. A twelve-foot alligator thrashed his tail. A tall, thin man grunted in the bouncing boat, his black hair tossed by the wind. He was all smiles, miles from the nearest person in the middle of the swampy Everglades. That's how he liked it: just him and his flashlight.

"You boys hungry? I've got a treat for you tonight." The man opened the box in his boat and pulled out another pound of fish. He then threw a dead chicken into the water. He grabbed another bag that contained animal blood and poured it over-board. He laughed at the sight and whispered, "Come get it, boys. Tonight is going to be a feast."

The alligators surrounded the dead animals and began to chow down. One swallowed the floating chicken in one swift gulp.

"Wait for it. Wait for it. Where's my death roll?" asked the man in the boat.

Two alligators started to fight over the feast. One larger alligator bit down hard on a smaller one and began a death roll, the method used to drown prey. The man threw his head back and let out a hearty laugh.

"Good boys, that's what I like to see. Now, since you've been so good, I brought you something special. Here's the real treat." The man looked around to make sure nobody was approaching. He was safe, as only the animals were out at 3 a.m. in the Florida Everglades. The man pulled the body out of the bag and threw it overboard. "Happy trails, Natasha. Better luck in your next life. If only you would have learned to shut your mouth. Have at her, boys."

As the alligators started to devour the body, the man turned on the engine and sped off through the water. He enjoyed the solitude. Gazing up at the stars, he was happy to rid himself of a major liability. It took him nearly an hour to arrive at the spot where he left his car, and another hour to hitch the boat. He looked at his watch. Wow! It was 5 a.m. already? He had to be at work early tomorrow. Five minutes later, he was driving slowly down the highway and back toward Miami. He knew not to speed at night, as the cops would love nothing better than to write a big ticket. The cops were a joke in this city. A cesspool of incompetence and corruption. He loved it. He was five minutes away from his apartment in Brickell, a hip spot near the water only a few minutes from downtown Miami.

He was nearly at his apartment when two drunk college students appeared. They were walking across the street and saw the boat attached to the car.

"Billy! It's a boat. Let's jump on that beast," said one of the drunk college students.

"Nice boat," said Billy. He could not stop laughing.

The driver got out of the car as the drunk students jumped up and down in it.

"Hey, jerks! Get off my boat." The man was six feet tall but thin, so the college students were probably not threatened by his appearance.

"Calm down, man. We just want to go for a ride. It's all good."

"Don't you idiots have anything else to do? It's early Monday morning. Don't you have a job or a class to go to? Why don't you get a job and do something with your pathetic lives? This is what is wrong with society. The youth of this generation just want to party all the time. They don't believe in hard work."

"Calm down, grandpa."

This made the man fume. His face turned red; his hands balled into fists. "Get off my boat. Don't make me ask you again. The light just turned green. I don't want to get hit."

"There's nobody on the road. Relax, dude," said Billy.

"I've had enough. Get off my boat or I will blow your brains out!" yelled the man. He pulled out a nine-millimeter gun.

"He's got a gun. Run!" yelled Billy.

The two college students jumped off the boat and dashed across the street.

"Aww. Where're you going? I guess you're not so tough once you see a gun pointed at your face. Run along now before I change my mind and kill you." The man adjusted his black hat and sunglasses. That would teach those punks a lesson.

The man got back into his car and arrived at his building five minutes later. Time to sleep. He had to be up in a few hours. Perhaps he should've done that on the weekend but, oh well, the deed was done. He pulled into the parking garage of his twenty-story high-rise.

2

STEVE JONES WALKED TOWARD HIS OFFICE AT SOUTHEASTERN University Law School, located in South Miami. This private school in sunny South Florida was the number one law school in the state. It was known for its rigorous academics and for having the top bar passage rate in Florida for the past ten years. The law school attracted many hard-working students looking to get an education. Steve was more than willing to exploit them all for the honor of working with him. He walked, almost skipped, through the halls as he planned to dominate the department's publishing output. He'd make them all look like lazy ingrates in comparison.

Suddenly, one of Steve's criminal law students approached. "Hello, Professor Jones."

"Hi. How's it going?"

"I'm ok. Thanks for asking, Mr. Jones."

"It's *Doctor* Jones. I didn't suffer through my joint JD/PhD program to be called Mr. Get it right."

"Sorry, Dr. Jones. Could I stop by your office today to ask some questions?"

"Uh, yeah, ok. Come during my office hours. I'm in meetings all day today."

"When are they?"

"Really? What are you, an idiot? It's called a syllabus. Look at it. Frigging memorize it. You mean to tell me I wasted my time putting it together? It contains all the information you need about my course and my office hours. You know when people say there is no such thing as a dumb question? They're wrong. There *is* such a thing, and it comes from dumb people like you. Please tell me that you aren't going to ask these types of questions in court," said Steve flatly.

The student's mouth hung open and before he could respond, Steve stormed off down the hall toward his office. He laughed to himself as he approached the door.

A voice rang out behind him. "Hello, Steve." It was another law professor. "How's the semester treating you?"

"Another day in paradise," said Steve as he looked at the students drinking coffee in the quad.

"I don't miss my days in Boston."

"Indeed. I don't miss the cold of New York either," responded Steve.

"Well, nice seeing you too, Steve. Try not to be too hard on the students today."

Steve was being nice for a change. It took real talent to be the biggest jerk in a law faculty. He won the prize by a mile.

He opened the door to his office. Home sweet home. He turned on the lights and went toward his bookshelves, which were filled to the brim with criminal justice and law books. Steve was an avid reader. On average, he read three books per week.

Steve heard a soft knock. My goodness. What did these people want? His job would be so great if there were no students. Maybe if he didn't answer, they'd go away.

A student knocked again.

"What? Come in." He wanted to move his office to a place where nobody could find him.

"Hello, Professor. Do you have a second?"

"No! My office hours are posted on the door in large font. Can't I have a moment's peace without one of you yapping in my ear about your problems? Goodness! Just read the textbook, do the assignments, and leave me alone."

Steve went to sit at his desk and turned on his desktop computer. His office didn't have a window. Prime real estate offices were reserved for senior faculty. Steve couldn't get along with the administration if his life depended on it, so they stuck him in a windowless office on the third floor of the law library.

"I'm sorry. It'll only take a second," said the student as she looked at the academic awards hanging on the back wall. "Wow, you have a lot of degrees."

The wall, full of accolades, forced everyone in the office to gaze at Steve's accomplishments.

Steve ignored the compliment, opened his email, and started reading. "Seriously, some people at this university have nothing better to do than send out emails every five seconds. Delete. Delete. Delete. What? Do you want me to answer emails all day or do my job?"

"Professor Jones, I just wanted to ask if you give study guides for the final," said the student reluctantly.

"Study guide? What is this, amateur undergraduate hour? No. I don't. Tough luck. Welcome to law school. One exam is your entire grade, so if you can't cut it, you won't be wasting anyone's precious time, including mine."

"I understand. I'm sorry for asking," she said and turned to walk away.

Steve, however, was not done with her. "You need to toughen up if you're going to make it in the real world. Lawyers are not nice people. They will eat you alive." Steve stared at the ceiling. He tended to do this when he pontificated. "I don't have a study guide. I've got a meeting with my research assistant. My advice is to read and study hard. Reading is when you drag your eyes across the page of a book. Often people like to go to the library. Just to let you know, the law library is located between Starbucks and Subway. It's the big building in the middle of campus. Come on! Start thinking like a lawyer. Nobody is going to hold your hand at this institution."

"Thanks, Professor Jones. Have a nice day," said the student on the verge of tears as she turned to the door and exited.

After deleting several emails, including those from students, Steve opened a folder on his computer that had all his works in progress. Steve was a prolific scholar and had published more than one hundred law review articles and several textbooks. When he started out as a law professor, he wrote all the law review articles himself. Three years into his academic career, he realized that he could exploit his smart law students who were eager to publish to bolster their resumes. Steve had three research assistants and a half dozen other students toiling away on articles at all hours.

He heard a knock at the door and without looking up responded, "Come in." A professionally dressed young woman walked into the office. Her name was Samantha, one of Steve's research assistants.

"Hi, Professor Jones. Do you still have time to meet about the article?" asked Samantha. She had a 3.9 grade point average and was the editor-in-chief of the law review.

"Yeah, I've got time. Grab a seat," said Steve. He started to brush his black hair with his hands. Regardless of his rude overconfidence, he was always fidgeting with nervous energy. This nervousness manifested itself in many ways, especially his inability to stop touching his hair.

"I'm done with the first draft, Professor Jones. I wanted to run a few ideas by you regarding the conclusions before I send it to you. I've also got to check some citations."

"Which paper is this again? I'm sorry, but I've been working with other students as well."

"It's on juvenile lifers."

"Right. Listen, send me the draft, and I will give you some comments. I forgot to put this meeting on my calendar, and I have a lot to do. I'm helping supervise several students at the university's legal aid clinic, and they need me to read over some stupid documents before they submit them."

"I'll send you the draft in another week or so. Does that work?"

"No, didn't you hear? Send me the draft now. The sooner the better. You need the publications. You'll be doing me a favor as well. I've had a slow year, as we had a tough time placing several articles. For this article, we need to strive for a better journal. Also, remember that you're trying to be a lawyer, not an activist. Make sure you keep this in mind as you proofread. The last thing I want to be associated with is a bleeding-heart activist. Those people make me sick, and they have no business in scholarship. Do you hear me?"

"I understand, Professor. I'm doing my best. I'm here to learn," said Samantha quietly, not quite meeting his concentrated gaze.

"Sure. That's what all my students say. You need to smarten up. I know students don't care about writing. You know how much crap I have to deal with, doing students favors, allowing them to publish with me? They just want to add lines on their resumes, especially embellishing their work with me. They want something to talk about during interviews. I'm doing a public service here."

"I love research. I really do."

"Oh yeah? Give me a break. You realize that nobody is ever going to read this article in the real world. The law school journals are popularity contests. They just publish topics that are in vogue.

My past experiences have taught me that a well-researched article on a dry topic does not get you published." Steve focused on Samantha's eyes with a penetrating look. "Don't forget that this is a transaction. Nothing more, nothing less. Understood? You're using my name to publish. Do you want to be a top legal mind and scholar, or some fly-by-night attorney? You want to be a top legal scholar, and you need me to help you with that."

"Understood, Professor. I'm thrilled to have the opportunity to work with you," responded Samantha, nodding firmly.

"I'm doing you a favor, so act accordingly." Steve brushed his hand through his hair.

Samantha stood still and stone-faced as she waited for Steve to close his mouth. But he was not done.

"Wait! How's the opinion piece coming along? I guess I'll have to change it from 'Professor Jones' to 'Professor Jones and my star student'." He winked as he picked up a pen and stuck it behind his ear.

"I haven't had time. I'm sorry. I've been focusing on our article."

"Are you kidding? It's seven-hundred words, not a doctoral dissertation. What a disappointment. Forget it. I will write the opinion piece myself. I knew this would happen."

"I can do it, Professor Jones. I'll work on it today after my classes."

"That's what I want to hear. And you better do it. If you can't handle something, just let me know. There're dozens of students clamoring for the opportunity. Luckily, the editor is my good friend, and I've been writing the occasional 'Professor Law' column for over a decade. Don't blow this opportunity. Got it?"

"I won't. I'd better get going."

"Yeah, you'd better run along now. Remember that I need a draft sometime today. I can work with something, but I can't work with a blank screen and so far, that's what you've delivered."

"Yes, Professor Jones," Samantha said. She shut the door behind her.

Steve chuckled to himself. He was a star around here. He made this place look good. He looked at his computer and opened his email again, writing a reminder to the same student. Before he could finish typing a "friendly reminder", he heard another knock at the door. "How does anyone work here?" he said aloud as he brushed his hands through his hair. "Come in."

John, an overweight student with patchy facial hair, poked his head through the door. He was another one of Steve's research assistants.

"Hi, Professor. How are you? Is it still ok to meet now? I wanted to talk to you about the edits that I made to your textbook."

"I really need to do a better job writing down these appointments. I haven't been able to do anything without being interrupted," replied Steve, annoyed.

"Would you like me to come back?"

"No, now is okay. I'm under a lot of pressure to turn in the edits to the press. Ninety-nine percent of academics turn stuff in late." Steve leaned back in his chair and rubbed his hair. "I've decided to be in the one percent and turn in things prior to the deadline. This makes the press happier to work with you."

"I just wanted to let you know that I finished everything. I added the ten new cases that you recommended." The student pulled out his laptop and placed it on Steve's desk. "Can I show you some of my revisions?" The laptop had a few smudges of dirt and grease.

"My goodness. Did you drag your laptop through the mud at a BBQ? This is the dirtiest thing that I've ever seen. Disgusting!" Steve grabbed for a wipe and started to clean the computer screen. "I'm going to have to wash my hands in bleach. Shape up son, you stink. And lose some weight. Why should I work with someone as sloppy as you? Is your work as careless as your lifestyle? I mean, come on, man."

"I'm sorry, sir. I've been working around the clock. I'm neglecting my hygiene and eating fast food to get my work in on time," replied John as his gaze fell to the floor.

"Sure, sure. Whatever. Excuses for days with you people. Alright, what about the analysis? Did you add a few thoughts here and there? Do you know why I wrote a textbook?"

"To add a line to your resume?"

"Are you stupid? You think a guy at my level cares about a resume? The main reason is money. This textbook is three hundred dollars, and I get a piece of that action every time I make students buy it. Every three years, I make some updates and keep the press happy."

"To answer your question, yes, I added the analysis. I made all the proposed edits in track changes so you can see them."

"Excellent. Send this to me ASAP. I will take a look and send this off to the press. I'm sure that they will be happy," said Steve.

"I'll need another few days to review and edit the writing."

"Prioritize it, then. I really want to use this new book the next time I teach this class."

"I'll send it to you in a couple of days. Could I ask you a favor, though?" asked John with a worried look on his face. He had nervous bowels, which made him feel gassy.

"Make it quick. I've got a busy day."

John had done all the work. The least that this jerk could do is listen to his second question. "Understood. Would you mind recommending me for a judicial clerkship? I'm applying to work with the same judge you clerked for."

"Why? He was the biggest jerk I've ever met in my life. He's also three hundred years old. Go get a job."

"I think that it'd help my resume," said John.

"Come on. What do you want to do?" asked Steve.

"I want to be a judge, Professor Jones."

"Yes, I'll write your letter. But I'm not calling that pompous jerk. I've avoided seeing him for decades. Now, run along. I'm busy. And send me the edits before I change my mind."

"Will do, professor. Thanks for your consideration." John bolted out of the office.

Steve did not care how hard the students had to work or whether they were affected psychologically by his abuse and exploitation. He believed that students should be thanking him profusely just for the opportunity to work with such a brilliant scholar. A few of Steve's former research assistants ended up in the hospital due to exhaustion, but he did not care. Steve did not accept any excuses; he even sent one research assistant an email the day she was discharged from the emergency room. Steve thought there was a price to pay for greatness. One more line on his resume helped feed his ego, and he was willing to do it at whatever cost necessary.

Finally, he could do some work. Steve put his hands over his head and leaned back in his chair, satisfied with himself. He put on classical music, opened a book, and began to read.

3

DETECTIVE CARLOS GARCIA GOT OUT OF THE CAR AND WIPED THE sweat off his brow. He was slightly overweight but handsome, with jet black hair and a charming smile. Carlos was a product and success story of Miami Dade County. His parents had moved to Miami from Cuba when Carlos was only ten. Carlos worked his way through college and went on to earn his master's in forensic psychology. He joined the police force and moved up the ranks quickly. It was not without its challenges, given the state of the police department, which was known for corruption and misdeeds. But Carlos was known for his hard work and integrity. Unlike many of his colleagues, he kept his nose clean. He stayed away from unprincipled officers and focused on his own cases and problems. This was his tenth year working as a homicide detective.

Carlos adjusted his aviator sunglasses and looked up at the blue sky. The South Florida sun was not always conducive to wearing a black suit. Miami was always hot, and his girth made it difficult to be outside too long. He grunted as he made his way into the high-rise building on North Miami Beach.

"They're in apartment seven-hundred-and-four," said the woman working the front desk.

Carlos took the elevator to the seventh floor and jogged to the apartment. He quickly opened the door.

"Hello, Detective Garcia," said one of the local police officers, who was busy collecting evidence.

"Good to see you, Detective Garcia. Wish it were under better circumstances," said another police officer.

"Hey, fellas. What do we have here?" asked Carlos.

"The victim is a forty-year-old Caucasian woman," said the lead officer on the scene. "Her name is Victoria Lane. She's a divorce attorney."

"Cause of death?" asked Carlos.

"Seems to be strangulation," responded the officer. He lifted the sheet covering her body. "We found her hanging from the ceiling. Her office manager called the apartment complex because Victoria did not show up for work for two days. The building manager opened the door and found her like this."

"Yo, Carlos. Where's your partner in crime, you know, the cowboy? He's always good for a laugh," asked one of the officers.

"He's stuck in court. I'll brief him when he's out," said Carlos.

Known for her stylish suits and sharp wit, Victoria Lane was a courtroom brawler. She battled hard for her clients. Victoria had always known that she wanted to be a divorce attorney. Her father had left her mother when Victoria was only five years old; he went out for a drink one day and never came back. Victoria's mother always used to joke that it must have been a great drink. She never forgot the trauma that this caused her and fought hard for her clients to receive a fair deal.

"I'd imagine that this lady has enemies. I've seen her name plastered on the billboards throughout the city," said an officer.

Carlos walked around the apartment. It was immaculate

and had a terrific oceanfront view. He took a deep breath as he stared out into the Atlantic.

"Married? Children?" asked Carlos.

"No. She didn't believe in marriage. I'd bet that working as a divorce attorney convinced her that marriage is overrated," responded one of the officers.

Carlos looked at the body. "This looks like a suicide. Did you find any notes?"

"No notes."

Carlos gazed around. "There is no sign of forced entry. Nothing appears to have been stolen. I'm going to contact her office. Maybe she had a boyfriend or someone that knew her well. Perhaps she was depressed, and the pressure of the job got to her. She seems to have everything anyone would ever want. Doesn't make much sense to me why someone like her would commit suicide."

"Detective, this looks like a run-of-the-mill suicide. Don't go crazy here, keep it simple. The crime scene unit is on the way and will dust for fingerprints. There is no forced entry. Nothing was stolen. There doesn't appear to be any foul play."

Carlos took a deep breath again and remained quiet for a moment, thinking. He finally broke the silence, letting out a quiet belch. "I agree. I'm out of here, guys. I'm going to head down to the victim's place of business. Dang, I'm starving, and I need a drink. I also think that I need a new suit. I lost half a gallon of sweat walking from the police station to my car. Let's go out for a beer sometime, fellas. It's been too long."

"See ya," said the officers in unison as Carlos left the apartment.

4

CARLOS LEFT THE DECEASED'S APARTMENT AND DROVE INTO THE first fast-food place he saw. He grabbed a burger and a large soda and continued to the law firm, driving as he ate. He parked and finished his meal. The Victoria case was a puzzle. Why would a successful woman like her just up and kill herself for no obvious reason? Maybe she was just lonely after years of working. What did this life really mean anyway? All the money in the world didn't make people happy. Carlos wiped his greasy mouth and walked to the law firm, stopping at the front desk.

"Hello, sir. How can I help you? asked the office manager at Victoria Lane's law firm.

"I'm Detective Garcia. I wanted to know if you had twenty minutes to talk about Victoria Lane."

"I'm Meagan. I'm the office manager. Let's go to the confer-ence room." She got up and showed Carlos to the conference room. "Can I get you some coffee?"

"I'm okay. Thanks though. Has Victoria always worked alone?" asked Carlos as he took a seat at the table in what Meagan referred to as the war room. It was a beautiful space of wood and leather. There were stainless steel jugs on the table surrounded by four glasses of water. There was a library as well, and a few boxes neatly stacked in the corner. The blinds were closed, which made Carlos feel quite relaxed and cozy.

"Yes. I've been working here for twenty years. Victoria was a free spirit. She always said that she went into solo practice because she didn't work and play well with others."

"I understand the feeling. Sometimes, I wish I was solo." Carlos adjusted his tie. He prided himself on his professionalism. Even though he hated wearing suits, particularly during the hot summer days, he always made sure that he was dressed for the job. This was a value that his parents had instilled in him.

Carlos noticed Meagan was fidgeting in her seat. Her eyes were glassy. She was quite shaken by the past events, which made Carlos suspicious. Maybe there was foul play?

"I can't believe that she's dead. I've worked here forever. What am I going to do now? She was the best boss I ever had," said Meagan. She pulled out a tissue and wiped her nose. Normally, Meagan was a beautiful woman who looked immaculate, with not even a strand of hair out of place. Yet today she was disheveled; her hair was an absolute mess.

"I can only imagine. I'm sorry for your loss. But I'm confident that you will find something. There is no shortage of lawyers in this town. I'm sure any law office would be happy to have you," said Carlos with a smile.

"I don't know. I do a little bit of everything at this job. Victoria paid me well and always treated me fairly. I worked at four law firms before coming here. They treated me like crap. I worked like a machine and was paid next to nothing. Victoria believed in empowering women. She pushed me to get my MBA and even paid for some of it."

"She sounds like a great boss. I had to fight tooth and nail for the police department to pay for my master's degree."

Carlos paused and thought for a bit. "Did Victoria ever receive any threats? Did any angry clients ever show up?"

Meagan poured a glass of water for herself. "Not really. Every once in a while, she would receive a letter calling her a homewrecker. Divorce is messy. Victoria always fought for her clients."

"No stalkers? Nobody ever showed up at the office seeking revenge? Any scorned lovers? Or maybe a crazy neighbor?"

"Never."

"Hmm. How well did you know Victoria personally? Was she romantically involved with anyone? What about her family? Any family members?" asked Carlos.

"Victoria didn't believe in dating. The job was her life. It's not what most people want, but that was Victoria. She refused to speak to her father, and her mom died of cancer several years ago. She was an only child."

Carlos leaned back in the chair. He rubbed his hands through his thick black hair. He was quickly running out of questions. "This doesn't make any sense. Do you think she was depressed? No family, no romantic interests, but maybe the job got to her?"

Meagan thought to herself. She looked up and to the right. Carlos felt sorry for her and thought it best to wrap up things. She wiped her nose once more and finally responded, "I don't know. She seemed liked a happy person. I know she sometimes had a hard time not taking work home with her. She represented some women who were in awful relationships with abusive men. You know the wealthy ones are the worst. Some of these doctors and high-powered lawyers think that because they're rich, they can get away with anything. But I don't think Victoria would commit suicide."

"Yeah. I figured that, but sometimes people are not what they appear to be. People can be strong on the outside but distraught on the inside. I've seen it many times. It makes you wonder if you ever truly know someone. We didn't find any evidence of foul play at her apartment. And she didn't leave a note or any clues."

Meagan frowned and suddenly broke down. Carlos really hated this part of the job. They didn't prepare you for this at the academy. He always said the same thing that seemed to work on everyone: men, women, and children. "It's okay to cry. You need to let it out."

"I've cried so much over the last day that I don't think I have any tears left," Meagan blurted. "Victoria wasn't just my boss; she was a mentor. I wish that she would've come to me or felt comfortable opening up if she was depressed."

"It's not your fault," said Carlos. "There's no way you could have known. I've put you through enough. I'm going to leave my card with you. Please call if anything comes up. I'm waiting to speak with the crime scene folks, but all signs indicate this is a suicide." Then he got up and headed for the door.

"What about the cameras in the building? Can't you ask the managers for the tapes?"

"The camera system was down the day that she was killed. Imagine that. The building managers said that they were conducting maintenance and upgrading the system. Even if there were cameras, the building is full of blind spots, and there aren't any cameras near her apartment." Carlos opened the front door. "I wish you all the best, Meagan. Thanks again for your time."

"Thanks, Detective. I appreciate it. I do hope you can figure this one out. This is just so upsetting. I still can't believe she's gone," said Meagan softly.

"I know. Take care of yourself. Stay strong."

5

Carlos was driving on the Palmetto Expressway with his partner, Wayne Briggs. They had worked together for four years. Wayne was like a fish out of water in Miami. Unlike Carlos, who was shorter, dark-haired, and chubby, Wayne was six feet four inches and two-hundred and twenty pounds of solid muscle. Even though he was in his fifties, he was built like a tank.

He was from Mississippi and had a thick southern accent. He stayed in Miami after being stationed at a military base in Homestead. He loved the sunny weather and enjoyed hunting and fishing in the Everglades. Wayne joined the police force after leaving the military, and he was partnered with Carlos. Wayne did not speak a word of Spanish, which was a real drawback in such a diverse city. Yet what Wayne lacked in language skills, he made up in discipline, grit, and congeniality. He was born to be a detective and loved his job.

"Carlos, can we stop off in Little Havana for a Cuban sandwich? I've been craving one for weeks," said Wayne.

"Sounds good, my friend. I could go for a *cortadito* myself."

"You mean coffee? It's all the same sweet crap to me. Anyway, Carlos, can I ask you a question?"

"Shoot."

"Why do you think I keep striking out with the ladies? I've been on five dates this past month. Five first dates, that is. They never want to go on a second date. I mean, look at me. I'm in pretty good shape. And I'm not a prick."

"Do you want the honest answer?" asked Carlos.

"Yeah, man. Give it to me straight."

"Where have these dates been?"

"Three of them were fishing and hunting in the Everglades. I caught this massive sucker on the last one, you should've seen it."

"What do you wear on the dates? Do you put on your camouflage suits and wear your cowboy hat?" asked Carlos with a smirk.

"Yeah, brother, you better believe it. You've got to dress for the job."

"And by hunting, do you mean hunting for pythons?"

"You know me too well. Those are good eating."

"So, a fun date for you is to hunt for a ten-foot python in the Everglades. The question I have is, how you convince these girls to meet you in the Everglades. They probably think that you are going to kill them there. I'd scold my daughter if she went on a first date with a guy in the Everglades." Carlos laughed and slapped the steering wheel.

"I'm trying to be original. I want to give those gals an experience they'll never forget."

"Try going to dinner and a movie. What about the beach?" Carlos pulled down his sunglasses and stared at Wayne. "I don't know if you noticed, but we're not in Mississippi. This is Miami, and you need to do what Miami people do. You really don't fit in this city. I'm telling you this for your own good, Wayne."

"What? Should I spend two hundred dollars on a dinner

that tastes like crap? Should I go dancing? I need to be completely wasted to do that. I guess you're right. Maybe I should take a break from the dating scene, buy some new clothes, maybe save up some money to afford these outings."

"You aren't listening, *hermano*," replied an exasperated Carlos, his Cuban accent coming out. "I'm not saying take a break from dating. Just take a break from python hunting. We can do that together. For now, take a lady out to a nice steak dinner or something."

Wayne said nothing. Eventually, Carlos pulled up at Havana Harry's. The two detectives got out of the car and walked into the restaurant. They were greeted by the usual host.

"Hello, detectives. You gentleman are looking sharp today."

"Howdy," Wayne said with his southern twang and a smile.

"Table for two, please," Carlos requested.

Carlos and Wayne noticed people were staring at them. Cops were not popular in Miami, especially in this neighborhood. The Miami Dade Police Department had a long history of corruption that many residents had a hard time forgetting. In the late 1980s, at least eighty people on the police force went to prison two years in a row for drug crimes and corruption. The most famous scandal occurred when the chief of police was involved in a drug trafficking scheme with members of Colombia's Medellín cartel. He helped cartel operatives traffic at least one hundred million dollars. There were rumors that the chief was close with Pablo Escobar, the ruthless leader of the Medellín cartel.

Corruption remained a major problem for the department. Carlos and Wayne tried to stay away from the corruption. They had to turn a blind eye on several occasions. Many clean-cut officers were killed, while others were forced to take bribes. Since Carlos and Wayne could not change the department, they chose to remain separate.

Despite reforms to the police, many residents continued to distrust the organization and refused to cooperate. This made the job of law enforcement more difficult, as the chances of solving a crime dropped by half after the first two days. The code of the streets was strong, and people feared retaliation if they spoke with the cops.

Wayne and Carlos walked to their table.

"Hello, gentleman," Wayne said to the people eating at the bar.

The group looked down at their sandwiches and ignored the officers.

"Heh, well, have a nice lunch, folks, great chatting as always," said Wayne. *Pricks, all of 'em.*

"Let's order. I'm starving," said Carlos.

"I guess they don't like my southern charm."

"Miami is not a friendly town to law enforcement, Wayne. Heck, it's not a friendly town in general. You've got to realize that. You're a long way from Mississippi."

"True. You can take the country boy out of the country, but you can't take the country out of the country boy. Also, you really can't beat this weather. Fishing and hunting all year round. I love me some fun in the sun."

The two officers ordered sandwiches, which arrived quickly. Carlos began to talk about the Victoria case as they ate. Wayne was as puzzled as Carlos. There was very little evidence to go on and even less to infer.

"Do you think there are any other cases with a similar outcome?" Wayne asked as he
took another bite of his sandwich.

"I'm not sure," replied Carlos. "We should try to figure that out. Maybe there is someone out there, someone highly proficient in killing and policing?"

"A former cop maybe? A former cop with a need to kill all

the single gals. She was single, right?" asked Wayne, his mouth full.

"Yeah, she was. Anything is possible at this point."

"Gosh, I love a good puzzle," said Wayne as he finished his sandwich. "Are you going to finish that?"

"Yeah. Get another one if you want, but you aren't touching mine," laughed Wayne as he lifted his sandwich to his mouth. "I think mine has more pork than yours."

"Why do you have to eat so slow? Every time I finish first, and I have to watch your slow ass eat."

"Tough. You should probably eat slower, stop wolfing down your food like an animal. Women don't like that, you know."

"Screw them, screw you, and screw your damn sandwich."

6

CARLOS GARCIA HAD MOVED UP THE RANKS IN THE POLICE department by working hard. He was not afraid to put in eighteen-hour days. His work ethic, however, had destroyed his marriage.

His ex-wife, Margarita, argued that Carlos put the Miami Dade Police Department before his family. The divorce crushed Carlos. His ex-wife moved to Los Angeles and took their daughter Ava with her. Carlos tried to visit at least once every three months, but Margarita always gave him great difficulty. Every time he wanted to visit she would berate him about not seeing his daughter. Carlos loved Eva, especially seeing her bright face enjoying a stack of pancakes. It broke his heart that she lived across the country. This pushed Carlos professionally, and he continued to bury himself in his job to overcome his depression.

Wayne had a more carefree existence. He was never married but had a long rap-sheet of failed relationships. Wayne was more resilient and adapted quicker to tragedy than Carlos. He accepted what he could not change. As an outdoorsman, Wayne knew that life would go on in light of any event.

Together, the two made a good team. They kept each other grounded and this bolstered their success.

Carlos and Wayne were called to a crime scene. They hopped in the car, and Carlos sped down the streets. Twenty minutes later, they pulled up and jumped out of the car.

"Detective Garcia and Wayne the cowboy," said a police officer working the crime scene. "Great to see you. Wish it were under better circumstances." He lifted the yellow tape blocking off the crime scene. "The body is over there, boys."

"Thanks, officer," said Carlos.

Wayne tilted his cowboy hat. "Thank you." He ducked under the yellow tape.

Carlos and Wayne walked over to the dead body. Half a dozen cops were swarming around the crime scene. The victim was a twenty-five-year-old male.

"The victim is Jared Tate," said the lead officer. "He's a local gang leader for the Six-Street Gang. Looks like multiple shooters. They pumped fifty bullets into him. Full metal jacket."

Wayne looked at the body and shook his head. "Dang. What a waste of a young life. I guess that's life in a gang."

"This is enemy territory. What was our friend doing here? What do we know?" asked Carlos.

"Who knows? The Six-Street Gang has been trying to move into this neighborhood, according to the Miami Dade gang unit. Another life lost to the streets," stated the police officer with a shrug.

"Anybody talking?" asked Carlos.

"What do you think?" asked the officer.

"I know the answer," responded Carlos.

"Snitches get stitches, son," quipped Wayne.

A least thirty people stood around the crime scene.

"Indeed, snitches get stitches," Carlos repeated. "I'll never understand. Someone died, a friend, a brother, a son. And nobody will say anything?" He got no answer.

Wayne and Carlos walked quietly around the perimeter. They could smell sewage. The quality of life in this part of town was horrible, and the detectives knew it. Desperation, trauma, and dire poverty helped fuel gang violence, drugs, and crime.

"You see anything, my man?" Carlos asked a young man.

"Naw, naw. We didn't see nothing," he responded.

"That's hard to believe. Somebody gets killed in broad daylight, and nobody witnessed anything. How do you expect us to solve crimes if the community won't talk?" asked Wayne.

"Nobody saw anything. But even if I had seen something, I wouldn't talk. We're living in a war zone; it's rough out here in the skreets. You don't know nothing, fat boy," said one bystander. He himself was fat.

Wayne held back a smile; he had to remain stoic.

"What if this was your brother? Wouldn't you want someone to solve the case? We can't do our job without any witnesses," responded a frustrated Carlos.

"That's not how things work here, son. We run these skreets. We don't need no po-po round here."

Carlos shrugged his shoulders and continued to walk around the perimeter. He approached a group of women looking at the scene.

"Any of you ladies willing to talk? We can speak at the station in a safe space. Nobody is going to know. Let me give you my card," said Carlos.

"We didn't see nothing. Nobody did nothing," responded one woman.

"Right," said Wayne.

Carlos and Wayne walked back toward the body. Carlos uncovered the dead man's face. "So, what's this? What did he die of? Old age? Maybe he died of natural causes?"

The group of women cackled, repeating the last few words over and over to themselves.

"Just give up. It's like talking to statues. These folks have

JONATHAN D. ROSEN & AMIN NASSER

their rules—the rules of the 'skreets' and I have it on good authority that the 'skreets are wild,'" said Wayne, trying to cheer up his partner.

Another officer approached the two. "Any leads?" he asked.

"Yeah, we cracked the case," Carlos smirked. "According to witnesses, this guy died of natural causes. I'm going to hit the streets and speak to some of my CIs." Carlos had built solid relationships with half a dozen confidential informants that fed him details about street-level crime.

"That's why they pay you the big bucks. In my opinion, it's a waste of time. Just another dead gang soldier. Carlos, stop working around the clock. Just think, you'll be ready to retire in another thirty years. And by that time, the city will only give you fifty percent of your pension. Another day living the dream, working for Miami PD," said one of the officers working the crime scene.

"Yes, sir," responded Carlos.

"Hey John Wayne. Sorry, I mean Wayne. You should've stayed in Mississippi. We're going to hit more than twelve hundred murders by the end of the year. You detectives will be lucky if you close thirty percent of the cases," said the officer.

"Keeps me employed. If I survive, I might retire and become a fishing boat captain," said Wayne.

Carlos and Wayne spent the rest of the day chasing down leads. Police work was not glamorous and required long days. They were willing to put in grueling hours, however, if it meant that they could possibly solve more cases and stop more senseless killings.

7

—————

"SHE'S GONE, CARLOS! SHE'S MISSING. WE HAVEN'T HEARD FROM her in a week."

"What happened? Who's gone, Missy?" Carlos asked his twin sister.

"Natasha is missing." Missy was crying hysterically. "My baby is gone."

"What? I'll be right there." Carlos picked up his coat jacket, hanging on the back of his desk chair at the Miami Dade Police Department. He turned to his partner and said, "Wayne, my niece is missing."

"What?" asked Wayne with a puzzled look on his face. "Hold on. I'm not going to let you do this alone. We're partners. I'm coming, too."

Carlos and Wayne did not even wait for the elevator. They ran down the steps toward the parking garage, sprinted toward the car, and jumped in. Carlos drove down the streets like a madman. They arrived at Missy's house in South Miami in record time.

Missy was waiting outside her home in the sun. She had a panicked look on her face and was hyperventilating.

Carlos and Wayne hopped out of the car.

"She's gone, Carlos. Who would want to hurt my baby?" asked Missy.

Carlos put his arms around his sister. "We'll get to the bottom of it, Missy."

"Please help me! I can't live without my Natasha."

"When's the last time you saw or heard from her?" asked Wayne.

"Hi, Wayne. I'm sorry, but I'm a mess." Missy put her hands on her head. "We usually speak every day, but she's been so busy. She's been interning at a law firm downtown. This isn't like her. She would never just disappear. Her friends at the law school told me that she hasn't been to class."

"What is the name of the firm where she's working?" asked Carlos.

"White and Scott."

Wayne took out a notepad and wrote it down. He adjusted his cowboy hat and wiped the sweat dripping down his forehead.

"She's still living at the same place, right?" asked Carlos.

"Yes. She's in Coral Gables."

"Does she have a roommate?" inquired Wayne.

"She lives alone. Who would do this to my baby? Why would anyone ever want to hurt her? She wouldn't harm a soul," replied Missy.

"We'll find her. Don't panic," responded Carlos. He hugged his sister.

Carlos and Wayne went inside Missy's house and spoke to her for an hour. Missy could not stop crying. Her husband had died in a car accident when Natasha was five years old. Natasha was Missy's only child ... and Missy was Natasha's best friend. Natasha told her mom everything.

Carlos and Wayne filed a Missing Person report and headed

to the law school to interview faculty, staff, and other students. They wanted to get to the bottom of this and find Natasha.

8

Professor Steve Jones walked into the classroom full of first-year law students. He set down his briefcase and adjusted his tie. "Hello, class. Who's ready for some fun today?" He pulled out his seating chart.

Steve, like many law professors, used the Socratic Method where they would question and prod students to analyze complex legal questions. He would call on students randomly, which kept his students on their toes. Some of his colleagues utilized a modified version of the Socratic Method. Not Steve. He grilled students and challenged them. He wanted to see them sweat, as he found it hilarious.

"Mr. Sean Woods. You're in the hot seat today."

"Cool," responded Sean.

"No. Say 'thank you'. Goodness, where's the professionalism? Anyway, I hope that you are as excited as I am. Mr. Woods, what were the facts of the case in *Blake v. Florida*?" asked Steve.

"Mr. John Blake was sentenced to life in prison without the possibility of parole at the age of fourteen. He committed murder and was tried and sentenced as an adult. His lawyer argued the case in front of the Supreme Court."

"Good. What was the legal argument?"

"There are like a number of arguments. But, um, the main one has to do with the Eighth Amendment."

"Anything else?" prodded Steve.

"No. It like had to do with cruel and unusual punishment. The courts like said it was like cruel and unusual punishment to send a juvenile to life in prison without any hope of ever being paroled."

"Stop saying like! Like. Like. Like. You sound like some bimbo. You need to improve your language. You can't use 'like' and 'um' every three words in front of a judge. I'm like, not, like, just calling you out, Mr. Woods. Do you hear how you sound? Like a buffoon, like everyone in this class. You need to think about speaking succinctly. You must sound smart and right now, you sound dumb. If I have one more student say *'like'*, my head is going to explode." Steve paced around the room. "Your generation writes law school exams like you were writing a text message. You need to shape up or you won't last a day in court."

"Sorry, sir," responded Mr. Woods. He gulped, wiping his sweaty palms on his jeans.

"Mr. Woods, you're not off the hook just yet." Steve grilled him about the case for another thirty minutes. He then moved to the next case, picking on the same student.

"Mr. Woods, can you tell me about *Frank v. California*?" asked Steve.

"Um. I, um—"

"Now the ums. *Frank v. California*, Mr. Woods. Please, do speak up."

"I didn't read that case, professor."

Steve walked around the classroom and stared directly at Sean Woods. If looks could kill, Mr. Woods would've been dead. "So, you're unprepared. As usual, I guess. Mr. Woods, there is a place called the library. It's a big building with books. It's not a nightclub on South Beach. I recommend that you spend more time in it. This is your first year, and you're already slacking off. I can't wait to see you in your third year."

"I'm sorry, Mr. Jones. I thought that this case was for next week."

"For the last time, it's *Dr.* Jones. I didn't suffer through my PhD program in economics to be a regular old mister." Steve noticed a student who had his head down on the textbook. "I guess I'm keeping some people awake. Imagine that."

A few students laughed. The student began to snore ever so slightly.

Steve bent down and yelled into his ear, "Wake up!"

The student nearly jumped out of his seat. "What? Yes. I'm so sorry. I haven't slept in days. I've been up all night, reading. I can answer any question."

"I'm so sorry that our class is interrupting your sleep schedule. Would you like me to get you a cup of coffee? Starbucks is right across the street. I'd be happy to walk over. If not, I can get a blanket and bring you a sippy cup."

"No, sir."

"Class, this is not nap time. What's your name?"

"Mark Jones."

"Jones? We are definitely not related." Steve looked at the student. "Can I ask you one honest question? Do you find the book serves as a good pillow? I wrote this book thinking that it would help students." Steve rubbed his hands together. "I never imagined that it could double as a pillow. I should go back to the publisher and ask for more money."

"I'm really sorry. It won't happen again, professor."

"Right. Let this be a lesson, class. You must always be prepared. If you were my employee, I'd fire you on the spot. Get used to being tired. Get used to being put on the spot. That's the life of a lawyer. You must be more like me, or else you'll fail." Steve adjusted his tie and walked around the room. "Do you know that I used to enjoy sending emails to the prosecution at midnight on a Saturday night? Most people are lazy and just want to enjoy their weekends. Not me. I'm willing to do whatever it takes to help my client win."

"I would've loved to have you as my attorney," said one student who was known as the class go-getter.

"Wow, what do we have here? Don't kiss my ass. You won't get extra points for it." Steve looked at the ceiling, which was something that he tended to do when he had a deep thought. "If you can ruin their lives by sending bombshells that throw a giant wrench in their case, you have won half the battle. I can't tell you how much joy it gave me to ruin someone's family life."

Several students started to yawn.

"Goodness, it's like tossing pearls before swine with you people. I wish I had better students." Steve rubbed his hands together. "There's one job in criminal defense: represent your client to the best of your ability. Mind games are a key part of it, and I'm preparing you for the real world. This is called strategy. Most people are lazy and aren't willing to do the work. Make their life a living nightmare, and you can bring them to the negotiating table. This is vital in criminal court where more than ninety-five percent of all criminal cases plea out."

Steve loved to hear himself speak. While students recognized that he was a true subject matter expert, they could not stand his belligerent personality. He loved to belittle students and show them how much smarter he was than them.

"You're ruthless," said another student.

"Glad you approve. However, I call it being smart. Most people want to live their normal, boring lives. Many of you are in law school because you want to make money and have the prestige of calling yourself a lawyer. I'm sure a percentage of you are here because you couldn't get into medical school. Now, let's get back to our next case. Mr. Woods, did you read *Slate v. Smith*?"

9

STEVE WAS FINISHING SCARING THE LIVING DAYLIGHTS OUT OF HIS students in criminal procedure. As the students packed up their laptops and books, Carlos and Wayne waited at the door of the classroom. Once all the students piled out of the lecture hall, Carlos and Wayne approached Steve.

"Professor Jones, could we speak with you for a minute?" asked Carlos.

"Good day, sir," said Wayne. He tilted his cowboy hat.

"Yes. How can I help you? Can we make this quick? I've got a busy afternoon," said Steve.

"Of course," responded Carlos as he wiped sweat off his forehead. "One of your students has gone missing?"

"I've got many students. I don't keep track of their personal lives. I teach two courses in giant lecture halls. My students are just a number to me. That's it. Nothing more."

"This student was your research student a year ago," said Carlos. "Her name is Natasha Garcia. She's been missing for a week."

"Natasha Garcia. Oh yeah. She worked with me on a couple research projects, but we don't really work one-on-one. I don't

36

keep in touch. I tell my assistants what to do, and they hand in the work. I didn't notice that she hasn't been in class. As I said, this is a giant lecture hall: look at it. This isn't kindergarten, you know. I don't take attendance. Show up. Don't show up. I don't care. But don't come crying to me when you fail my class." Steve turned toward Wayne. "You're not from around here, are you?"

"No, sir. I'm from the great state of Mississippi," responded Wayne.

"Great? Not sure I'd call it great, but beauty is in the eye of the beholder." Steve turned and stared at Carlos. "I'm sorry that I can't be of more assistance. I don't know where Natasha is. I hope that you find her soon because she owes me some work."

"Understood. We're going to talk to some of her classmates. We just wanted to ask you if she seemed off, or if you heard anything," said Carlos.

"Haven't you been listening? I haven't heard anything, but I don't keep tabs on these people. They're all adults. Hey, you look familiar. Did you go to South Miami High?"

"I did. I remember you as well. Small world. I think that you were two or three years older than me, right?" asked Carlos.

"Yeah. I graduated in 1999. Did you play sports or something? Were you a star jock?" asked Steve, looking him up and down.

"I played football. Defensive back, to be specific. We went to the state championship and lost to Miami Senior High. I played in college for a year at Florida State, but I tore my ACL my first year. I could never make it back to full strength."

"And you decided to join the boys in blue? Seems like a classic Miami story. A jock becomes a cop. Maybe you could have been more original, Detective." Steve started to smile.

"No offense taken. If we could get back to the issue at hand," responded Carlos.

"I didn't mean it like that, Detective." Steve folded his arms.

"Listen, it's nice to talk to you boys. I wish that I could be of more help. Maybe she had a jilted lover? Maybe a stalker? Hell, what do I know? If I hear anything, I'll be sure to call you."

"Please do," responded Carlos.

"Take care now." Steve walked toward his office, determined to stay calm. Why would they want to talk to him? Steve took deep breaths as he sat in his office and thought about Detective Carlos Garcia. He was sweating. He recalled the night he'd killed Natasha and how he fed her body to the gators. No body, no murder.

Steve calmed down a bit and let out an enormous sigh. He didn't think he could survive in prison. He wasn't built for the inside. He would have to pay protection money or have his cheeks busted, as they say. He needed to calm down; he couldn't think like that. They had *nothing* on him. He was just her professor.

Carlos and Wayne walked around the campus and spoke to a few of Natasha's friends. They headed back to the station without any leads. All of Natasha's classmates had nothing but wonderful things to say about her. She was well-liked and popular. She made the law review her first year and became the president of the Hispanic Student Law Association.

"I vaguely recall Steve and even now he gives me a weird vibe. Always did. He comes across as an arrogant jerk. He was a loner in high school for that reason. His students sure do dislike him," stated Carlos.

"I agree. He seems like a real egomaniac. But if we arrested every egomaniac in Miami, there would be only a few people left," responded Wayne.

10

_____

"HI, PROFESSOR JONES. IT'S ASSOCIATE DEAN WALKER'S administrative assistant. Do you have time this afternoon? She'd like to speak with you."

"What do I owe this pleasure to?" asked Steve. He spun around in his office chair and admired his academic degrees.

"Are you free at 2 p.m.?" asked the administrative assistant.

"I guess I don't have a choice. Although I'd rather watch paint dry than talk to our wonderful law school deans."

Jane Walker was the arch nemesis of Steve Jones. Jane went to Yale Law School and graduated top of her class. She clerked for a Supreme Court justice and then became a law school professor at Columbia University. She was recruited to Miami to become the Associate Dean, as she was a leading tax scholar. Her colleagues loved her and described her as a terrific leader. Jane was humble and listened to her faculty. To top it off, she won several teaching awards. Steve hated her and cursed under his breath whenever her name was mentioned.

Steve despised anyone that got in his way or made him look bad. He viewed himself as a top legal mind in the field. Jane's success and ability to rise through the ranks faster than him annoyed him to no end. She was a full professor and was being recruited to become a law school dean at various universities. Steve was an associate professor with tenure, but his colleagues kept denying him the coveted full professorship. Jane served on the promotion committee and had been involved in the denials. Steve had applied for promotion on three separate occasions and was rejected every time, despite his scholarly accomplishments.

Steve walked into the associate dean's office. "I'm here. I didn't bring my lawyer, but I probably should have."

"I'll let her know that you're here." The administrative assistant walked into Jane's office. "Professor Jones is here."

"Thanks for letting me know. Send him in," directed Jane.

Steve glared at the administrative assistant and headed into the associate dean's office.

"Hi, Steve. Grab a seat."

"Thanks so much. How's life on the dark side? Did you figure out a new assessment form that the faculty should have filled out? I really don't know how you do what you do."

"I love my job, Steve. It's not for everyone," said Jane matter-of-factly.

"You used to be a respected scholar, Jane. Now you spend your days spamming my email inbox. But I'm glad you feel like you make a difference."

"It's not about me, Steve. We've had more complaints from students. Where do I begin? Have you read your teaching evaluations? You need to respond to them in your professional development plan."

Steve looked at Jane with disgust. He was insulted that someone would bring up his teaching evaluations. "My students are morons. They just want a good grade so they can clerk for a Supreme Court justice. Tough! I'm not going to lower my standards."

"It's not about lowering your standards," said Jane. She took a deep breath and closed her eyes for a brief minute. "Students have complained about your conduct. You've made inappropriate and degrading comments."

"Sue me. Our students need to toughen up. My parents were both lawyers and abused me verbally during my entire childhood. I know what derogatory comments are. Trust me." Steve began to rub his hands through his hair. "Have you ever been to a courtroom? Oh, right. You're a tax attorney. You figure out ways to shield billionaires from paying taxes. I'm glad your law degree is paying off."

"Steve, it's okay to be demanding, but you need to be respectful to our students. I've received dozens of complaints this semester. There're over a hundred faculty members here, and you give me the most trouble out of all of them. And I don't mean this as a compliment."

"I'm sorry my little snowflake students are offended. I've stepped foot in a courtroom. You need to be tough to be a lawyer. What is this Mickey Mouse nonsense?" demanded Steve.

"We've had students complain that you are not behaving ethically. We love that you want to work with students on publications, but there is a right way to do this."

"Excuse me. Is this personal? Are you just jealous that I still publish? The last thing that you published was a fifteen-page email on how we should format our annual reports." Steve leaned forward and crossed his arms. "I respected you when I first met you. I thought that you were a serious scholar that could change the discipline."

"Please don't raise your voice. And what a load of nonsense. You've always treated me like I was subhuman."

"How have I behaved unethically? I'm giving my students the opportunity to publish in law journals," said Steve.

"The students say that you don't even read the articles, let alone write them. They also complain that you demand that everything must be completed in unrealistic timelines." Jane leaned back in her chair. "I've received at least seven complains from former and active research assistants."

"Give me a break, Jane. They should be happy I'm willing to work with them. This is disgusting. I don't appreciate you attacking me."

"I'm not attacking you." Jane took a sip of water from a half-filled water bottle. "Several students have gone to the dean. The dean is tired of receiving complaints and has asked me to deal with it."

"I can deal with it by telling my students to grow up. They should be honored to work with me. I'm done here. I don't have to listen to this from a paper-pusher." Steve got up and stormed out of the room. Who did she think she was?

11

THEODORE BLAKE TOOK OUT THE TRASH. HE WALKED DOWN THE driveway of his single-family home. He'd moved to Naples, Florida after retiring from Southeastern University Law School, where he spent forty-nine years. Naples was quieter than Miami. Theodore lived alone, as his wife died three years earlier. He did not have any children which, at times, made him feel very lonely but he stayed busy volunteering in the community and playing golf.

Theodore closed the garage door behind him after taking out the trash. Suddenly, he felt a rope around his neck.

"Remember me, old friend? Let's go inside and have a little chat." Steve pulled the rope tighter.

Eighty-five-year-old Theodore was no match for Steve. Theodore gasped for air. Steve started to tie Theodore to the couch.

"I can't breathe," said Theodore. He was turning ghostly white, not only from the rope around his neck but from the horror of seeing Steve in his home.

Steve pulled out the duct tape and started taping Theodore to the chair. "If you make one sound, I will kill you. Understood? I'm not going to tape your mouth shut just yet, as I want to have a quick chat. Is that alright, Teddy ol' boy?"

Theodore nodded. He was sweating profusely. "I'm going to have a heart attack. Come on, Steve. I'm an old man. The past is the past."

Theodore was one of the most popular professors at Southeastern University Law School. He was on Steve's tenure committee and pushed hard to deny Steve tenure. Steve had a stellar list of publications, which impressed other members of the committee. Theodore observed several classes that Steve taught. He believed that teaching should matter, not just research. He viewed Steve as an engaging lecturer but arrogant. Theodore also harped on the several negative reviews in the student evaluations. Ultimately, Theodore lost and Steve was granted tenure. The other committee members were impressed with Steve's strength in quantitative methods and his PhD in economics from a leading university made him a real asset.

Steve's tenure case was kicked up to the dean and later the provost. They thought that not granting Steve tenure could hurt recruitment and morale. Steve was recognized by the provost on several occasions for his research. Steve later found out that Theodore was the one behind the scheme trying to jeopardize his career. After receiving tenure, Steve never spoke to Theodore again.

"I can see that you are doing well, rotting away in Southwest Florida. You're a shell of your former self. You look terrible. You got fat and old." Steve walked around the chair. "I've been waiting so long to come after you. You really screwed me and made my life a living hell. I lost so many nights of sleep thinking about what would happen if I did not get tenure. I would have had to start over. Do you know how difficult that is in this market? Of course not, you have no idea. You were just jealous of me."

Theodore started to squirm in the chair. "Please, Steve. I'm sorry. Let's be adults here. We can work this out. I was wrong, I should have supported your bid."

Steve pulled out a knife. "Wow! Look at you squirm. Did you think it would come to this? I've been waiting for so long to get my revenge, and it has finally come. I should have done it years earlier. I want you to suffer after all the pain that you have caused me. You made me suffer for so many years."

Theodore realized he was about to die. He decided to go out with some dignity. He'd lived a good life and was a man of principle. Theodore took a deep breath and responded, "You're a narcissistic jerk. Always were. I spoke with the associate dean a few years ago, and she told me that you are unbearable. The provost should have listened to me. It turned out I was right. What happened to you to make you like this? Did your parents screw you up? Do you have mommy issues?"

"Adults go to people directly, not behind their backs. You trashed my reputation at the law school."

"No! *You* trashed your reputation, Steve. You became a pompous jerk who treats your students like garbage. You're so talented. Nobody denies it. You think that you're never wrong, but that's not true."

"Enough!" yelled Steve. He plunged the knife into Theodore, who fell to the floor. Steve took a deep breath and started to smile. He stood over Theodore's lifeless body and said, "That felt so damn good."

Steve put on his gloves. He spent hours cleaning up. He wanted to make sure that he did not leave behind any DNA. Steve prided himself on trying to outsmart the cops. At 2 a.m., he loaded the body into the car. The neighborhood was full of retirees and nobody was awake at this hour.

Steve drove across Alligator Ally, a long and flat road that connected Naples to Miami. He pulled off halfway across Alligator Ally, put his boat into the water and drove out into the swamp. He opened a black trash bag, which contained pounds of dead fish. He took out another bag that contained pints of blood.

"You boys are going to love this. It's going to be the biggest feast that you've had in nights."

Five alligators, each bigger than ten feet, swam toward the blood. Steve quickly threw Theodore's remains into the water. "Not the way you wanted to go, Theodore. But it feels so good to watch."

Steve turned his boat around and made it back to his apartment by 5 a.m. "Home sweet home," grinned Steve as he opened the door.

His one-bedroom apartment was immaculate. Steve walked into the bathroom and turned on the shower. He let the water run down his body and thought about tonight's conquest. Revenge felt *so* good.

12

STEVE WOKE UP AT 6 A.M. HE PUT ON HIS JOGGING CLOTHES AND laced up his running shoes. He ran at least four times a week. The blistering sun meant that he either ran early in the morning or at night.

He ran around the water for an hour, thinking about Natasha and the talk he had with Carlos and Wayne. After a quick shower and shave, he went to his local diner and ordered a Cuban coffee and breakfast. This kept him energized until he needed his afternoon coffee with cream and sugar.

After preparing for his lecture, Steve went to the law school.

"Hello, Professor Jones. Great piece," said one of his students.

"Glad you liked it. Hair analysis is BS. I bet you didn't know that they have convicted people using dog hair. Did you?"

"I didn't," responded the first-year law student.

"You should. Now, run along."

Steve walked by a faculty member named Bart Smith. He was an emeritus professor who still showed up every day. His wife had passed away, which kept this eighty-eight-year-old professor coming to work to stay busy. Bart was one of a handful of faculty members whom Steve got along with.

Steve and Bart engaged in a ten-minute conversation. Bart always treated Steve with respect and praised his excellent scholarship. This was the main reason why Steve liked him so much. Bart got along with everyone and was the quintessential, jovial old man. Bart took the time to read Steve's law journal articles. He would stop by Steve's office and let him know what he thought of the articles. Bart would tell Steve that he was changing the field and would often say, "You're a star young man."

Bart was one of Steve's only friends on the campus. Steve's other colleagues avoided him like the plague. Outside of law school, Steve was a loner. He did not have any friends. He did not date. Steve had married at the age of thirty, but the marriage lasted for only one year. His wife, a contract attorney, began to loathe Steve. When they were dating, Steve pretended to be a nice and romantic guy; after they got married, Steve became more controlling and was obsessed with proving to everyone that he was smarter than them.

The divorce crushed Steve. His ex-wife remarried, and Steve vowed to never date again. He grew to despise women and told anybody who would listen what a terrible person his ex-wife was.

Moreover, Steve did not have any siblings. He was the only child of Deborah and Rick Jones. They were criminal defense attorneys in Miami. They worked long hours chasing money. Both parents drank too much and abused Steve both physically and emotionally. His parents died young in a house fire, believed to have been started by cigarettes, while Steve was away at law school. The authorities speculated that his parents were both passed out drunk.

* * *

Steve opened the door to his office. Before he could sit down, Maria Sanchez knocked on the door. Maria was a visiting assistant professor, often referred to as a VAP. She earned a three-year appointment after graduating from law school. She wanted to be a law professor, but the legal market was saturated. Finding a tenure-track job at a law school in a major city was an uphill battle. Given that law professors in general had a less stressful life than practicing attorneys, many people wanted to go into teaching. The hours were better, and the pay was not bad.

The VAP position gave Maria a chance to experience teaching and work on her scholarship. It was rumored that the law school was going to open several full-time teaching positions over the next two years. If Maria could keep up her solid teaching evaluations and publish three more articles, she would be a competitive candidate.

"Hi, Steve. Is this still a good time?"

"Come on in. Glad we can chat." He leaned back in his chair. "I wanted to ask you a favor."

"Sure. What's up?"

"I've been invited to present a paper at a conference. Would you mind covering a class for me?"

"Criminal law?"

"That's the one," said Steve.

"When?"

"In two weeks. I'm sorry to keep asking you to cover my classes. If you do this, I'd be happy to write you a letter of recommendation. The rumor is that three new tenure-track professorships are going to open up."

"I'm sorry, Steve. But I'm supposed to give a talk at a nonprofit downtown."

"Cancel."

"Excuse me?"

"Cancel. You can give the talk anytime. Do you really want

to make me angry? I'm going to fight like tooth and nail to get onto the hiring committee. I don't want to have to say that you are uncooperative and a terrible colleague." Steve looked disheveled. "I'm a well-known scholar in the field. Trust me, you don't want me on your bad side. I also have a really hard time letting things go."

"Okay, Steve. I can teach your class. I'm sorry. I don't want to have any issues with you."

"That's the spirit, Maria."

"What material are you covering?"

"Cover whatever you want. Seriously, I don't care. I just need a warm body in the room." Steve picked up a book. "Thanks again, Maria. Way to be a team player. The law school needs people like you."

Maria considered going to Human Resources, but she didn't want to create problems and ruin any chances of receiving a full-time position. Becoming a professor in the city that you already lived in was like hitting the lottery twice. These things just did not happen in academia, where hundreds of applicants would apply for an open position regardless of location.

Maria would later learn that Steve did this to new professors, visiting professors, and a handful of senior fellows. The new faculty knew that Steve was well-known in the field. What they did not realize was how much the administration hated him and, therefore, avoided putting him on any hiring committees. Steve had been on one hiring committee after receiving tenure and made the candidate cry during her job talk.

13
―――――――

CARLOS SAT AT HIS DESK AT THE MIAMI DADE POLICE
Department. He was reviewing his notes when the chief of
police came over. She had been in the job for three years. She
rose her way through the ranks and had strong ties to the
Cuban community. After serving as the deputy chief of police
in Los Angeles for four years, Denise Vargas made it back to her
hometown. She was brought in to clean up things.

The Miami Dade Police Department was dealing with low
levels of trust among citizens. Prior to Denise taking the helm,
there were half a dozen cases of the police being caught on the
payroll of criminal organizations. Four officers were sentenced
to twenty years each for their involvement in a kick-back
scheme. Finally, there were several sexual harassment lawsuits
brought against the department by female officers. They
argued that the department was a toxic work environment for
women.

Despite her five-feet-four-inch stature, Denise was tough as
nails. People used to call her Ms. Napoleon behind her back, a
title she secretly liked. While some officers resisted the change,

JONATHAN D. ROSEN & AMIN NASSER

she was respected in the department. She was shaking things up and wanted to get rid of the bad apples. And the Miami Dade Police Department had plenty of bad apples. Some experts and outside critics argued that Denise should start from scratch.

"Carlos, I heard about your niece. I'm so sorry," said Chief Vargas. "Any leads? I hate asking this, but are you sure that you can handle this case? I'm tempted to pass it along to Ramirez and Smith. You know the rule about working on cases involving family. It's too close and personal for an officer."

"I can handle it, Chief. Please keep me on the case. I want to get to the bottom of this. My sister is devastated. She needs an answer."

"Okay. But there's a reason why doctors don't operate on their own family members. It's personal, and they lose objectivity." The chief looked at Wayne, whose desk was next to Carlos' desk. "I'm counting on you, Wayne, to keep him level-headed. Understood? I want to make sure this is crystal clear, or I'm coming for you. And you know I'm fierce."

"Roger that, Chief Vargas. I'll keep this boy in check and make sure he doesn't do anything foolish." Wayne may not have fit into the Magic City of Miami, but he was the consummate professional. Not only was he tough as a rock, but he believed in the system and chain of command. Wayne had seen it all in the military, including several soldiers end up in prison for breaking the rules.

"Excellent. I'm glad we have an understanding about the ground rules for this case. Now, who would want to harm your niece?" she asked, regarding him closely.

"Nobody. She doesn't have any enemies. She has spent her whole life trying to help people."

"Any boyfriends?"

"Nope. She's been focused one hundred percent on school." Carlos took a sip of lukewarm coffee from a chipped mug and turned to the chief. "I've interviewed some of her friends and classmates. The only problem that she had was with one law professor. She worked for this guy as a research assistant. Natasha went to Human Resources to report him. It was an anonymous complaint."

"For what?" asked the chief.

"This guy is a jerk. He exploits his research assistants to write articles for him. We went to high school together. I didn't know him well. He's an arrogant prick but aren't many law professors known for being tough?" he asked, frowning.

"I'll refrain from making my lawyer jokes," said Wayne.

"Keep your nose to the grindstone. I want you boys to keep me posted. I don't want to be in the dark," instructed Chief Vargas.

"Roger that," said Carlos.

"Whatever you say, Chief," echoed Wayne.

"And remember to get some rest. Carlos, you look like garbage and you're starting to smell. Go home. Shower. Shave. We need you sharp. I can't have you running on fumes."

"Will do."

Carlos continued to put in long hours despite the toll on his health. A triple homicide case last year had landed Carlos in the hospital. He slept in the office for a week. He then passed out one day at work. The doctor said that he needed to rest and take care of himself. If not, he was destined for an early grave. His cholesterol and blood pressure were already high due to poor eating habits and stress.

Carlos and Wayne spent another two hours at the office before calling it a night. They decided that they were going to keep a closer eye on Steve. This would require good old-fashioned police work. Carlos was known for his patience. On the other hand, Wayne liked the fast-paced action that he was accustomed to in the military.

Carlos and Wayne walked out of the police station and to their cars. Even though it was 9 p.m., it was still eighty degrees.

"See you in the morning, Wayne. Rest up, my boy."

"You, too. The chief is right. You do look terrible."

"Thanks. I guess."

"Be safe, bud."

14

STEVE NEEDED A BREAK FROM MIAMI. SINCE HE DIDN'T TEACH ON Fridays, he decided to head to New York for a week on Thursday night. He wanted to escape the heat as well as take care of some pending business. He landed at John F. Kennedy International Airport and took a cab to his hotel in Union Square. The city had some great restaurants and bars. He also loved New York's history of crime and murder. As a lawyer and killer, it was his favorite place.

Steve wandered around the city for hours. He loved getting lost amidst the concrete jungle. Steve walked by his old stomping grounds, passing by the apartment that he lived at near Washington Square Park, close to New York University Law School. He walked from Washington Square Park all the way to Central Park, and then had dinner at a famous steakhouse noted for its connection to organized crime. Steve often daydreamed about what it would be like to work with the Mafia; those people knew how to reward loyalty. He could be so wealthy ... if he just knew someone. After a hearty meal, he retired to his hotel room. Tomorrow was going to be a busy day.

* * *

The next morning, Steve was up at seven and grabbed breakfast at one of his favorite local diners. He took the train to the Metropolitan Museum of Art and spent several hours there. At 3 p.m. he entered Mark Vince's apartment, a high-rise building in Tribeca. He walked through the lobby, nodded to the security guard, and entered the small elevator. It shook as it struggled to get to Mark's floor. Steve hid in a blind-spot and waited for Mark to return home.

Steve had met Mark Vince when he was at NYU Law. Mark was the chief editor of the law review, a prestigious position at a top law school. Steve had served as an editor as well, but Mark tried to have Steve kicked off the journal, as he accused Steve of stealing his ideas. Mark confided in Steve about an idea that he was toying with; Steve adapted the idea and ended up publishing a paper with another law school professor before Mark. Mark took the case to the administration. A hearing was held, but there was not enough evidence to prove that Steve had stolen Mark's idea.

Yet the damage was done. Mark did everything in his power to blacklist Steve. He told his friends and colleagues, making it nearly impossible for Steve to intern at a prestigious law firm during the summer of his second year. The news got around that Steve was not to be trusted, and Steve had to fight hard to restore his reputation.

Mark became Steve's mortal enemy and Steve vowed to get revenge. After graduating from law school, Mark went to work for Prat, Thomas, and Smith, a multi-national law firm that specialized in corporate law. He spent several years billing ninety hours per week. The long hours took a toll on his health and personal life. He was thin, and his eyes were sucked up into his skull. He managed to survive the miserable first few years and became a partner. Yet he was divorced by age thirty-five.

Sad and alone, he buried himself in his work, trying to find meaning in what he felt was a meaningless life.

Mark walked toward his apartment building at 9 p.m. after a long day of meetings. Distracted, he did not notice anything peculiar as he drew close. He strolled past a figure without any thought and got his keys out of his pocket. Mark opened the door and Steve punched him in the back of the head, pushing him into the foyer. Steve slid a rope around his neck and tightened it. Mark was on his knees, confused, as Steve placed a trash bag over Mark's head.

"I'll kill you if you scream. Don't test me," instructed Steve.

Mark was gasping for air. "I can't breathe. Please! Stop! Who are you? What do you want?"

"Nice place you've got here. I'm glad your fancy law degree paid off." Steve led Mark to a couch in the living room.

Mark did not recognize Steve's voice. He had not seen Steve in fifteen years. Steve had always been patient and hadn't minded waiting years before seeking revenge.

"Grab a seat." Steve took off the trash bag from Mark's head.

"Steve! What do you want? I haven't seen you in decades."

Steve tightened the rope around Mark's neck. "Let's have a little chat, my old friend. I wanted to catch up with you. It's been so long." He looked down at Mark. "Man, you look like absolute crap. You look emaciated. Do you want something to eat?"

"What do you want?" repeated Mark. He was beginning to sweat. The rope around his neck cut him, and his breathing was labored.

"I'm not sure that you knew that I landed on my feet, despite your efforts to ruin my life." He took a knife out of his pocket and ran the tip down Mark's cheeks. Steve noticed the lines on his face. "What are you, thirty? Forty? You look like you could be sixty. What happened to you? I'm pretty healthy. I make the effort to keep in shape."

"Please, don't hurt me. What do you want? Law school was a long time ago, Steve, please."

"I know. I became a law professor. I'm a leader in my field. I have tons of books and articles. My students love me and fight for my attention. I can't get a moment's peace."

"I heard. That's great. I'm happy for you. I always knew that you were smart. I just thought that you played fast and loose with the rules, that's all. It was a long time ago ..."

"Fast and loose," Steve interrupted. He swiftly cut Mark's cheek and blood started to run down his face.

Mark screamed in fear. "The past is the past!" he yelled. His eyes were wide, welling up with tears. "Please, what are you doing? This is stupid. Do you want to go to prison over this? I won't say anything about this if you leave now."

"Oh, Mark. You must think I'm stupid. Look, you're not going to make it out of this apartment alive. Unlike most killers, I'm smart. I know the law, forensics, all that mess. And the cops? Cops are stupid jocks that don't have the brainpower to figure out things."

"All this must be a dream. This *must* be a joke."

"Nope. I'm *dead* serious. No pun intended." Steve started to laugh. "I've killed dozens of people. Mainly people who have wronged me over my life. You know I was once married, Mark?" Steve looked at Mark with a penetrating stare. He held the knife up to Mark's jugular. "Her name was Vanessa. She was an attorney, like me. We got married after I started teaching in Miami. She ruined me. She remarried and was happily married for sixteen years until her death."

"You killed her?" asked Mark. "Why? I'm divorced. Life goes on."

"I grew to hate Vanessa to my core." Steve held the knife tighter against Mark's jugular. "She went to a work conference in Arizona and her car fell off a cliff on a winding road. It was a rainy night and the cops thought it was an accident. They were too stupid and lazy to realize that I gave her car a gentle love tap. What a tragedy."

"You're a murderer. You're a real monster, Steve."

"I know. I know, but I can't stop killing people. I get such a rush doing it, especially getting even. It feels good, you should try it sometime. I must have killed thirty-five people over the last ten years. Sometimes, I kill random strangers who have wronged me. Mostly I kill for revenge and the thrill of it."

"You're a terrible person," Mark said, trembling.

"I try." Steve slapped Mark in the face, pulled away the knife, and tightened the rope around Mark's neck. "I waited sixteen years for revenge. Vanessa ruined me. It felt so good watching her car fall off the cliff. Her poor husband was devastated. I think his name was Chris or Bob or something. The cops later found him dead from a heroin overdose. No one knew he used drugs. It was a real shock. Fun little fact: I killed him too. I just popped him with a needle. Easy."

"What do you want, Steve?" Mark was sweating profusely. "Do you want me to apologize? Is it money? Do you have financial problems? What can I do to get out of this?"

"Revenge is what I want. Now, let me tell you what I'm going to do. I'm going to feed your body to the rats. Mafia hitmen used to do this. The cops will never look in an abandoned tunnel on Long Island."

Mark started to squirm in his chair. Steve pulled the rope tighter. "But first I need you to do something for me. You need to write a little note."

"No way!"

Steve punched Mark so hard that he fell back onto the couch. Steve then pulled the rope so tight that Mark did not have a choice. Steve handed him a pen and a piece of paper. Mark wrote a suicide note with his hands tied. He wrote that law made him miserable. Money was not the only thing that mattered. He missed his wife and hated himself so much that he wanted to disappear.

"Let me see," said Steve.

Steve used gloves to avoid leaving any fingerprints. He had become an expert on crime scenes and learned from the mistakes of past criminals. "Looks pretty good. You always had a way with words."

"Wait! I'll pay you. I can also apologize," said Mark. He looked at Steve and started to cry. "Do you want me to invite you to give a talk at my firm? I'll do anything ..."

Before Mark could finish his statement, Steve plunged the knife into his stomach. "You animal," hissed Mark, as the life went out of his body.

Steve spent three hours cleaning up. He stored Mark's body in two large suitcases. Steve rolled down the suitcases and put them into Mark's car, which was parked on the third floor of the parking garage.

Steve drove to the town of Hempstead on Long Island. He found an abandoned train track. Garbage covered the ground, and the stench of death and decay permeated the air. This was a good spot for that swine. He looked around and, seeing no one, dumped Mark's body there. Steve then walked a few feet away and hid behind a rusty car, waiting for the rats to come.

"Enjoy the feast, my greasy friends. I brought you some good vittles. You guys deserve it," Steve said aloud to the dozens of rats scurrying around the train tracks. He laughed to himself, remembering how Mark begged for mercy. Serves him right. Steve hoped Mark would enjoy being rat food.

He drove back to New York City and put the car back in the garage. He had to hurry to catch his flight. Steve rushed back to the hotel, got his things, and headed back to the airport to catch the plane to Miami.

Steve learned from other serial killers that crossing state lines made it harder to be tracked. The police had a difficult time recognizing patterns. Mark would just be another dead lawyer in New York. Steve had read dozens of books on serial killers who were caught because they killed similar victims within a small radius. Steve's motto: if you wanted to be evil, you had to be smart about it.

As Steve boarded the plane, he felt enormous relief. After years of hatred and frustration because of Mark, he had finally rid the world of a source of pain. He reclined in his chair and looked out at the New York skyline. After letting out a sigh, he wondered if the rats were finished with their meal. He imagined a pile of bones picked clean. What a weekend, Steve thought to himself as he sat on the airplane. Revenge was so sweet.

A stewardess interrupted his thoughts and requested he put his seat in the upright position. Steve did not like her tone. His happiness turned into anger. He reluctantly positioned his seat and looked outside the window. He hated this world. If he could kill her right now, he would. Steve never enjoyed the catharsis killing brought for too long. Something, or someone, would always bring feelings of inferiority that provoked murders. The nameless stewardess did not know how lucky she was.

15

CARLOS AND WAYNE TOOK AN INTEREST IN STEVE AND BEGAN TO track him. The complaint that Natasha brought against Steve made them suspicious. They met with various faculty members as well as current and former students. Steve's current research assistants all said that he was an arrogant jerk. They believed that he used his academic credentials and power to exploit students. It seemed clear to the detectives that this was indeed true. It was not uncommon for this to occur in academia, as it was a cutthroat world. Carlos and Wayne told all the students that they were just trying to get to the bottom of Natasha's disappearance. They did not want to tip off Steve that they were tracking him.

Carlos and Wayne met with the associate dean, Jane Walker. They arrived at her office around 3 p.m.

"Come on in, detectives," said Jane. "I wish we were meeting under better circumstances. As you can imagine, we're all devastated by Natasha's disappearance. Would you like some coffee or water?"

"Thanks, Dean, but nothing for us," said Wayne as he

grabbed a seat next to Carlos. "Terrific office. I've never seen so many law books in my life."

"Please call me Jane. No need for all this 'associate dean' stuff."

"Thanks, Jane. We don't have any suspects. We're just trying to get to the bottom of this. Can we speak with you about Professor Steve Jones?"

"You mean Professor Law?"

"Professor Law?" asked Wayne.

"Steve fancies himself as a public intellectual. He writes opinion pieces under the name Professor Law."

"That's right. I've read some of his pieces in the paper," said Carlos as he scratched the stubble on his chin. "I enjoyed them. He always writes interesting, sometimes humorous articles. We actually went to the same high school."

"He's a smart guy, but a difficult person. But there is no doubt that he is smart."

"Oh yes, we met him. Jane, we wanted to ask you about Steve. Natasha was a research assistant for him. We learned that she filed an anonymous complaint with Human Resources, is that correct?"

"Yes. They contacted me and the senior leadership at the law school. Natasha is not the first person to file a complaint." Jane leaned back in her chair. "Steve is not the only professor in the world to utilize students to do the heavy lifting for scholarly works. It's the way that he treats his students that annoys them. Frankly, he abuses them."

"I'd be annoyed writing papers for someone else, but especially for someone like that," said Wayne.

"You've never spent much time around a law school, right? We've got students who are driven to excel. They're happy to have the opportunity to publish with faculty. Believe it or not, Steve is a big name in the field."

"Is there any reason for Steve to feel threatened by the students?" asked Carlos.

"Threatened? He's a tenured professor. It's almost impossible to fire him. Yes, he's a jerk, but being a jerk is not illegal, Detective. I'd love to get rid of him, but I can't. I don't have anything else to tell you. I've got a meeting coming up. You've got my contact info. Email me or call anytime. You have our full cooperation. We want to find Natasha. She's a star student and a great person."

"Thanks, Jane. We appreciate it."

Carlos and Wayne walked around the campus for another hour. They knew that Steve had a class in the afternoon and decided to follow him. They tracked him the rest of the evening. Steve went running around and grabbed groceries at a local supermarket. He then spent the rest of the night in his apartment.

"This guy is a creep, but he lives a normal, boring life," said Wayne. He tore off the wrapping paper of his hamburger. "Nothing seems out of the ordinary."

"He's just another jerk professor who thinks he's never wrong. I've got a gut feeling that he's hiding something. We'll catch him when he slips up. I know he will."

16

STEVE HAD BEEN LAYING LOW IN MIAMI FOR WEEKS. HE KNEW that Carlos and Wayne were following him. He made sure that he was home every night by 8 p.m. He would read until midnight. Steve enjoyed his own company and loved to read. He was always a homebody. He used to tell himself that maybe prison would not be so bad. If he was locked up, he could read all day and would not have to deal with law students or faculty. He would have all the time in the world. Of course, he was just lying to himself. Steve had to take a tour of a prison facility during law school. Inside, prisoners yelled—always screaming about something.

While Steve was taking notes, a prisoner screamed in his ear for him to move. Startled, Steve jumped backwards. The other prisoners laughed at him. He looked around in fear and backed up into the bars of a prison cell. A prisoner then squeezed his buttocks. Steve quickly turned around and the prisoner said, "Do something, lil bitch." Steve backed away slowly and continued the tour. After that experience, he knew he would not be able to survive in prison. Steve thought that he had an amazing life and did not want to jeopardize it. Deep down, he wanted to stop killing but was addicted to the sense of relief that was attached to the act of ending someone's life. As long as he was smart about it, he wouldn't get caught. The police were dumb, and he was smart.

* * *

On a cloudy Wednesday night, Steve traveled to Philadelphia for a law conference. He was going to present a paper on a panel about juveniles spending life in prison without the possibility of parole. Steve knew the topic like the back of his hand. However, he had to read the paper on the airplane, as his student wrote ninety-five percent of it. Steve wanted to make sure that he was prepared for any questions. He made little notes in the margins to remind him of facts or arguments.

Steve checked into the conference, which was held at the convention center in the heart of Philadelphia. The conference had more than three thousand law professors and students presenting their research. There were a lot of people there, and they'd come to see him.

Steve walked to the book display. He had a meeting with the acquisitions editor at a top university press. He spoke with her about a book proposal. He had an idea for a new and innovative book. Steve looked flawless on paper, and he knew how to manipulate people. He charmed the editor. She told him that the press would love to review his book proposal and send it off to peer review. He pretended to be humble, thanking the editor for the once-in-a-lifetime opportunity.

Steve walked around the conference and listened to a few panels. He thought they were fools. He ran into a few colleagues from different universities. They viewed Steve as a serious scholar and were happy to see him. While Steve treated his students and nearly all his Miami colleagues like garbage, he treated the superstars in his field like royalty. He knew how to charm them. If only they would have known his true personality.

Steve presented his paper three hours later. He told the audience that it was impossible to talk about this topic in fifteen minutes, but he would do his best. He received terrific comments from the panel discussant and audience members. Steve loved the attention, which strengthened his perpetually fragile ego.

The conference, however, was not the real reason Steve had traveled to Philadelphia; it was just his alibi. He had been tracking Emily Rivers, a former high school classmate. She had lived in Philadelphia for the past six years, and Steve wanted to pay her a visit. Steve hated Emily with a passion, as she'd spread rumors about him in the past. Emily told people that Steve was a freak. She told other students that Steve had a bad home life and tortured animals to relieve stress. Nothing too specific, just typical teenager nonsense. However, it was more than that for Steve. He was jealous of Emily. To him, she had it all: beauty, brains, and popularity.

Emily disliked Steve because he was a jerk to her. They had four classes together in the first two years of high school. Steve enjoyed competing with Emily and picking apart her ideas in class. He hated that she had it all. Steve had longed to be noticed in high school. He thought that people would think he was smart if he could take down Emily.

Emily went on to college and became a financial planner. She graduated from the Wharton School of Business at the University of Pennsylvania. After working in San Francisco for nearly a decade, she decided to come back to the East Coast. Long hours and stressful jobs took a toll on her personal life. She was engaged once, but the engagement did not last. Emily was not a very happy person and she struggled with her work-life balance.

Steve stalked her and found out she was living in a

rowhouse in Fishtown, a trendy neighborhood in Philadelphia. She lived alone with her cat, Ruffles.

Steve went back to his hotel and changed into a hoodie and baggy jeans. He did not need a suit for the type of job that he was about to perform. Steve not only excelled at blending in but also in planning and execution. He had tracked Emily for years. Tonight was going to be the culmination of many nights of deep brooding and careful thought. And he had the perfect plan.

He was going to disguise himself as someone looking to move into one of the apartments for rent in her rowhouse. He spent countless hours trying to determine the right time to kill Emily. Now that the police were watching him in Miami, he knew that this conference in Philly would be his best chance.

* * *

Even though Emily had lived in Philly on multiple occasions, she did not know many people in her neighborhood. The neighborhood was up-and-coming and had people moving in all the time. People stuck to themselves. At times, Emily became depressed that she did not have a closer network of friends. Several of her close girlfriends got married and had kids. They only had time for Emily once every six months. They were so busy with their lives that Emily had to drive out to the suburbs on the mainline just to have a quick cup of coffee. It was so tiresome.

Emily was financially successful and bought the entire building. She rented out two apartments. Two of her tenants decided to move out within the same period. One couple had lived there for six years and bought a house in the suburbs, as they were expecting a baby. The other couple lived there for four years. But when the wife's job was transferred to Los Angeles, the couple decided to move across the country.

* * *

Steve approached the row house. He had on a wig and wore a Phillies baseball hat under his hoodie. Steve also had on a fake nose. It cost him nearly three hundred dollars, but it made him unrecognizable. He was confident, nervous, and excited all at the same time. His fake nose held on to his face regardless of the sweat pouring from his forehead on that hot and humid night.

Steve rang the doorbell, heart pounding. He could feel the adrenaline rushing through his body. He jumped up and down, excited to get the show on the road. He loved the thrill of the kill.

The door of the rowhouse opened. "Hello. Nice to meet you. I'm Emily. You must be Bill."

"That's right. Hi, Emily. It's great to meet you as well. Thanks for agreeing to show me the apartment on a Sunday. It's hard for me during the week, as I've had to travel for work."

"No worries. Come on in. Do you travel a lot for work?" asked Emily.

"I do. I've got some pretty big clients in the Midwest. I sell sandpaper products."

A tenant who was never home. She liked this guy already. She took Steve to the second floor and opened the door of the apartment.

"Wow! It's very spacious. And what a great location. I love the neighborhood. It has changed so much. I went to college in Philly, but before that, I worked in Chicago for a decade. When I lived here years ago, this was a rough part of town. Lots of drugs and crime."

"The neighborhood is great. I bought the building a few years back. I love it here. I looked at a place in Northern Liberties, but I liked it better here. It reminds me a little bit of Williamsburg in Brooklyn."

Steve pretended to be interested in the apartment. He looked through the kitchen drawers and nodded his head. Confident, Emily turned her back to walk into the master bedroom to check the ceilings. She had removed a small amount of mold and wanted to make sure it had not returned.

Steve quickly put a gun to her back. "Don't make a sound, or I will kill you."

"Oh my gosh. Oh my gosh." Emily started to cry. "Please don't hurt me. I'll give you whatever you want. My wallet is in my apartment. I have some jewelry."

"Shut up. Do you think I need your shit? Let's take a walk to your apartment." Steve held the gun to Emily's back. They exited the apartment and walked up a flight of stairs to Emily's place.

"Not a bad spot," said Steve as Emily walked through the door. "Stinks of cat urine. You've turned into a cat lady. Go and sit on the couch."

"Don't hurt me. Please! Just tell me what you want. I'll do anything."

"I want you to suffer." Steve pulled off his hat and wig. He then removed his nose. "Surprise! It's me. Do you recognize me?"

"Steve? *Steve Jones*? What? Why?" Emily started to cry.

"That's right." He pointed the gun directly at her face. "You're not so tough with a gun in your face, huh?"

"Please don't kill me. What do you want, Steve?"

"I never understood why you went so far in high school to ruin my life."

"That was such a long time ago. I shouldn't have spread rumors. I was just a stupid kid. I'm sorry for writing the blog posts."

"Are you really? You screwed me up so bad." Steve walked closer to her and placed the gun to her forehead. "Do you know what I have that you don't? Don't answer. It's a rhetorical question. I'm patient. I've been waiting for the right time to get back at you."

"I'm so sorry. Don't kill me. How will you live with yourself?" Emily started to cry uncontrollably. "I can't change the past. But I want you to know that I'm sorry. I was young and immature. It wasn't right."

"You don't feel sorry!" yelled Steve. "You're just begging for your life."

"Please. Please. Don't kill me."

Steve forced Emily to get up and walk to the bathroom. He filled the bathtub full of water. Ruffles the cat poked his head out from under the couch. He looked at Steve and let out a tiny meow.

"Take your clothes off and get in."

"Don't do this, Steve." Emily could not stop sobbing. "I don't want to die."

"Do as you're told, *now*," instructed Steve.

Steve pulled out the hairdryer from under the sink. Emily had a long enough extension cord to reach the bathtub.

"No! Don't do this to me, Steve."

"Any last words?"

"No, please. I'm sorry. I'll make it up to you, please. I'm too young to die," yelled Emily.

"We're never too young to die." Steve threw the hairdryer into the bathtub and watched Emily fry to death.

Steve spent another hour cleaning up. He walked one last time to the bathroom. "See you later," he said to Emily's lifeless body.

Steve put his disguise back on and let Ruffles out. The poor cat looked back at his owner, and then up at Steve. Steve smiled and shooed the cat out of the apartment. Steve then walked several blocks to a different part of Fishtown and hailed a taxi. He wanted to rest before his 5 a.m. flight back to Miami.

17

CARLOS AND WAYNE WERE FINISHING UP WHEN THEY WERE interrupted by another murder call.

"Carlos, are you and Cowboy Wayne done messing around?" asked a senior officer on the police force. "We need you boys in Miami Beach. Now! Chop chop! There's a dead body."

"Roger that. Be there in forty-five. Hopefully, there isn't too much traffic," said Carlos.

"Let's go, brother." Wayne chugged the rest of his coffee. "Time to roll."

After some time sitting in traffic, Wayne and Carlos arrived at the scene. An officer lifted the tape and let the two detectives in.

"Move aside. Miami's finest cops coming through. The body is in the trunk of the car," announced the officer.

"What is animal control doing here?" asked Wayne.

"Ha! You're going to love this." The officer took out a hand-kerchief from his back pocket and wiped the sweat off his fore-head. "Geez. The heat is killing me."

"Animal control? Hello?" asked Carlos.

"Oh right. Sorry, I can't think straight with the heat. There's a cottonmouth in the trunk," responded the officer.

"Go get some water, and when you are ready to be a professional, come back," shouted Carlos.

"Carlos, a cottonmouth is a snake. Those things are poisonous," explained Wayne. He adjusted his cowboy hat, proud of his knowledge of wildlife.

"You're telling me, Cowboy Hat," responded the officer with a wink.

Carlos and Wayne walked toward the vehicle. A rookie cop approached them. "You want to see the snake?"

"As long as it's in a cage or whatever," replied Carlos pensively.

Carlos and Wayne looked at the body. The victim had rope marks around her neck and various puncture wounds where the snake bit her.

"What does the snake have to do with all this? It looks like she was strangled. Check out her neck; see those strangulation marks?" Carlos pointed out to Wayne.

"Yep. It's so obvious," said Wayne. He looked around and asked, "Any identification?"

"Her name's Linda Green. She's a lawyer. Well, she used to be a lawyer," said the officer. He walked around the car. "Our friend Linda here retired last month. She's divorced. No kids. She lived in this building."

"Another lawyer who happens to be single," said Carlos to Wayne.

"Like Victoria," responded Wayne.

"Who would want to kill her?" Carlos asked the officer.

"That's why we called you folks."

The two detectives spent three hours at the crime scene. The building was old. Half of the tenants were snowbirds who escaped the northeast during winter. The homeowner's association did not want to pay the extra five hundred dollars a month per tenant to upgrade the security system. Consequently, the building had no working cameras and the security guards were too busy drinking and watching TV. Another guard was in his eighties and frequently napped on the job.

* * *

Steve Jones and Linda knew each other, as they had worked on several criminal cases together. Steve wanted to gain more experience in criminal court after becoming a law professor. He never spent time working full-time as a private attorney. Linda needed an academic type on her defense team. She thought that judges would be impressed with a JD/PhD sitting next to her in the courtroom. She and Steve had worked on fifteen cases together.

Linda and Steve won several cases. It was not unusual for Linda to partner with other lawyers. She believed in volume. She did not want to put all her eggs in one basket. She liked working with Steve not only because he was smart, but he was confident; he was not afraid to work hard. She was impressed with Steve's ability to strategize. It gave her great pleasure when Steve would send a bombshell 3 a.m. email on a Saturday night to the prosecutor. Steve used to tell Linda, "We need to overwhelm them with paperwork and ruin their weekends. The prosecutors are already overworked. They just want to do their time and become judges."

Steve and Linda worked together like this for years. Then, one day over coffee with a soon-to-be-fired secretary, Steve learned that Linda charged more than four times the rate she paid Steve. The secretary was already disgruntled because Linda would not pay her on time. Linda cheated Steve out of hundreds of thousands of dollars. He confronted Linda about this, and she told him that he was being paranoid. Steve then found out from the consultants he knew that Linda was indeed underpaying him. Steve had his doubts, and he had to know for sure.

One night, he broke into Linda's office and found the billing records. He was astounded. The next day, he visited Linda's office threatening to sue and file a report to the bar association. Linda laughed Steve off, which only infuriated him more.

Linda had a serious gambling problem; as soon as she received payment, she went straight to the casinos in Fort Lauderdale. She left for the casinos when she finished work and then spent three to four hours playing Blackjack. That was then. She retired young to focus full-time on gambling. Her defense was that she could not pay Steve back even if she wanted to. The truth was, Linda desperately needed "to get back into the game" (as she would say). Eventually, she revealed to Steve that she was broke, that gambling had taken much of her nest-egg. She would add, "I feel my luck changing for the better and no one can stop me, not you, not even the bar association."

Steve waited years to act on his impulses regarding Linda. He knew that after his angry display at her law office, he would be a prime suspect. He bided his time and waited patiently. Linda retired and devoted her life full-time to gambling. Steve would often follow her to the casino and watch her gamble away *his* money. Of course, Steve could simply sue, but he knew Linda had no money. Steve understood it was futile, but he had his thoughts on other matters. He couldn't get blood out of a stone, but he sure as hell could get blood out of her.

Ultimately, Steve got his revenge. He killed Linda in a planned affair. He threw the cottonmouth in to throw detectives off track. It was purely symbolic: Linda was a gambler in life, and she lost millions. She got *snake eyes* in life and in death.

Another name crossed off on his revenge list—a growing list.

18

STEVE WAS DENIED A PROMOTION TO FULL PROFESSOR AGAIN. HE wrote several threatening emails to the dean, who refused to meet with him. The dean told Steve that he could discuss the case with Associate Dean Walker.

Not being promoted to full professor was a cause of great irritation for Steve. A salary increase and the new title would have been nice. Yet Steve had tenure, making it very difficult to fire him. If he only knew how to play the game—even just a little. His teaching evaluations were horrible, and his colleagues could not stand him. In his mind, these issues were not enough to deny him full professor twice. Given his status and publication record, he was a shoo-in for the title. It was clear to him that this was personal.

Steve walked into the associate dean's office. He looked disheveled, as he had not shaved in days. Part of his shirt was untucked and his black hair was a mess.

"Hello, Professor Jones," said Dean Walker's administrative assistant.

"I'm here for my meeting with Associate Dean Power Trip. Sorry, I mean Walker."

"Dean Walker is expecting you."

"Right."

Steve walked into Jane Walker's office and sat down.

"Hello, Steve. How've you been?"

"How do you think?"

"How can I help you?" asked Jane.

"You know why I'm here." Steve scratched the facial hair on his chin. "Why was I denied the full professor promotion again? What do I need to do? What does this university have against me? Sure, some snot-nosed kids don't like my classes, but I'm a leader in my field. I mean, what's wrong with you people? Is it too much to ask to promote me to full professor?"

"I know you must be disappointed," said Jane with little emotion.

"Stuff that robotic crap back where it belongs. I know how happy you are that I kept getting denied for promotion. You just want me out of here and out of your hair. Without me, this law school is nothing. I publish more than anyone on this entire damn campus. The last person who published anything was some assistant professor who wrote a book review in a tier-two journal. I know what goes on around here, unlike you."

"Nobody is questioning your academic production." Jane took a sip of coffee. She needed to maintain her composure, as she did not want Steve flying off the handle while in her office. "There is more to promotion than scholarship. Your evaluations are terrible. And your service is almost non-existent."

"I'm a great teacher. Students are in line to publish with me. My classes are always packed to the rafters. The problem is that I'm tough. This generation is weak. They won't be able to survive out there. The real world is tough. This isn't kinder-garten; no one cares about how you feel, or if you live or die. Half of my students would get eaten alive in a courtroom." Steve rubbed his hair, pulled at his shirt, and jerked his neck. "Jane, do you want me to tell you what a courtroom is?"

"Please don't patronize me, Steve."

"Oh, what do you know? You're a paper-pusher and an ass-kisser. Typical bureaucrat. You've made zero contributions to the field and have never litigated an important case in your life. The difference is that you know how to play the game and ingratiate the right people to move up the administrative ladder. You don't get to decide my fate. Only I do."

"This is not about me, Steve. We can end this meeting now if you're going to keep attacking me."

"I deserve to be a full professor, Jane. This university is lucky to have me. You should be on your knees, kissing my ass right now."

"Please be respectful. If you're not happy, you can always go on the job market. You seem very confident in your abilities," responded Jane coolly.

Steve stared at her with a penetrating look. "Can't say I'm surprised that you're divorced. You're a soulless monster."

"You're on thin ice, Steve. Do you want me to report you to HR? We're done here."

"This law school needs me. Someone here must publish. Not everyone can sit in boring meetings all day, except you. I bet you get off on it. I'm not ever leaving this university. I don't care if you deny me my promotion. You'll have to kill me first." Steve got up from his chair and stormed out of the office.

* * *

Jane sighed loudly and noticed that she was trembling. She quickly opened a file on her computer titled Steve Jones. The dean told her to report all interactions and incidents with Steve. If they ever wanted a chance to fire him, they needed to build a case. She had compiled fifteen pages of notes. The university counsel had informed them that being rude to colleagues and students was not grounds for termination. The university administration, however, would keep tracking all incidents and wait for Steve to slip up. All Jane had to do was build a case. She happily typed up her notes.

She couldn't wait to get that prick out of there once and for all.

19

STEVE WAS IN A FOUL MOOD ALL DAY. HE LOOKED A MESS AS HE drove to South Beach. When he needed to escape, he would go for a drive, park his car, and walk for hours. Steve parked his car on Ocean Drive, a hopping place on South Beach right on the Atlantic Ocean. Washington, Collins, and Ocean Drive were populated with bars, nightclubs, and restaurants. Steve had a drink at each one. Silently he slurped on fancy-looking cocktails with fruit piled high, people-watching. He overheard some conversations that made him sick to his stomach.

"I love you so much," a young man told his girlfriend. "I'm so glad we decided to come to Miami for the weekend. I really needed to get out of the cold."

That made him want to puke. A year from now, they'd be divorced. He'd seen it a million times. Steve hated seeing couples happy. His divorce made him hate all relationships. He kept walking and saw other couples sharing food and drinks.

Why were these people so happy? Did anyone work in this city? It was Wednesday night, not Saturday. They should go home and read a book, or maybe find a hobby.

Steve continued his walk down Ocean Drive and saw more

couples laughing at the bars and restaurants. He hated seeing people have a good time. Steve was smart and had a job that gave him endless amounts of freedom. Best of all, it was nearly impossible for him to be fired. Yet he was still not happy. Steve wondered if he had ever been happy a day in his life.

Steve's parents lived to work and never thought about his mental health and well-being. As an adult, Steve realized that he had many characteristics of his father, who had an inferiority complex. His father worked hard. He was smart, but not a genius. He often felt inadequate and needed to prove to people how great he was. This led him to work insane hours and live an ostentatious lifestyle. It was important for people to know that he was a big deal. He would wear three-thousand-dollar suits and fancy watches to impress other lawyers. Steve, like his father, was never satisfied. Steve was less into material objects, but he wanted people to know that he was smart. He loved telling people about his long list of publications and how many scholars read his work.

Steve walked around for nearly two hours. He went back to his car and drove down an alley to cut between two streets. He heard a thud and got out of the car to see what it was. *What did I hit? I hope I don't have a flat tire.* As he inspected the tires, a young male in his twenties popped out from behind the trash can. He was holding a large knife.

"That's a nice car you have there. Give me your wallet and the keys, or I'm going to cut you up into pieces."

"Yeah, right, kid. Go back home to mommy." Steve looked at the young man with an evil stare. "I'm not giving you anything."

The young man moved closer to Steve, who was near the trunk of the car. "I'm not going to ask again. Give me your wallet and the keys, or I'm going to kill you."

"Oh, okay. Give me a second," Steve pulled out a gun from his waistband and shot the young man in the stomach. "I'm the wrong person to mess with. And this is Florida. Everybody has a gun, idiot. Try Vermont next time."

Stunned, the man looked at Steve and collapsed in a heap. Steve threw the body in the trunk and sped off.

People at a neighboring restaurant heard the gun shot and came running.

"I don't see anyone," said a local busboy.

"Me neither," responded a waiter.

Steve gripped the steering wheel of the car tight and started to yell, "That's what you get when you mess with me! Don't mess with Dr. Steve Jones. You hear that, Jane. I'm coming for you!"

Steve drove to an abandoned warehouse in North Miami Beach. He put the body in a barrel and drove away. The young man Steve had killed was a local runaway. He had struggled with drugs and was homeless for several years. He had a long rap-sheet and had been to jail at least half a dozen times. In the last six months, he started stealing cars, then selling them to a chop shop in North Miami.

The following night Steve drove back to the Everglades, which was his favorite dump site. The Everglades was crawling with alligators and large pythons. It was a perfect place for a serial killer to dispose of bodies. Steve also had a soft spot for these predators, and he was happy to feed them the flesh of those he thought unworthy of life.

20

STEVE WALKED ACROSS CAMPUS AND POPPED INTO THE LOCAL coffee shop. A student waved at him. Steve looked and gave him a nod. It was Howard Ross, a joint JD/ PhD student. He jogged up to Steve.

"Hey, boss. You want anything?" asked Howard.

"Black coffee would be great, and a croissant."

Howard grabbed the coffee and walked over to the table where Steve was sitting.

"Nice to see you, Dr. Jones. Thanks for meeting with me."

"How's the paper coming along?" asked Steve. He did not see any reason to beat around the bush with pleasantries. "I need our paper to be published in the top journal on crime and law. I reviewed the statistical model that you sent me. Did you get my comments? I have a few questions regarding how you coded several of the variables."

"I'm almost done. But I wanted to talk with you candidly."

"Oh yeah? About what?" Steve sipped his coffee. "Is something wrong?"

"I just don't think that it's fair for me to do all the work and be the second author. You've written fewer than two pages of the paper. Would you mind if I published it on my own? This is the third paper we're doing together, and your contribution has been minimal, to say the least."

"Really? It's my idea, Howard. All this is possible because of me."

"I could thank you in a footnote."

"Howard, Howard, Howard. This is not how all this works. You do realize that I'm on your dissertation committee? Do you want me to fail you?" Steve looked at a noisy group of laughing undergrads. "You'll submit the paper with my name."

"My friend's dad is on the board of trustees. I've been thinking about talking to him."

What Howard did not realize was that Steve believed in having leverage on all his teaching and research assistants. Steve loved plotting revenge and spent hours digging up dirt in case this type of situation happened.

"That's too bad, Howard. I'm disappointed in you. Is this how you treat others? Are you treating me like you treat your lovely wife? Oh, and how's your wife doing? Isabella, right?" Steve pulled out a folder and opened it. "We do a lot of bad things in secret, but everything comes out eventually. Take a look. I see that you've been hanging out with one of your students. You know that it's inappropriate to have a relationship with a student when you are the teaching assistant? That's no good."

Howard looked at the photos of him with a second-year undergraduate student. He started to panic. Cold sweat ran down his now pale face.

"Seems like you and Ms. Taylor here were doing a little more than studying," said Steve with a quick smile.

"What do you want? I'll do anything you ask," replied Howard. He leaned into the table and lowered his voice. "Please don't tell my wife. Isabella would be crushed."

Steve knew Howard's wife, as she was also a law student.

While he did not know her well, she had taken several of his classes.

"It's so simple. What I want is for you to hold up your end of the bargain." Steve took another sip of coffee. "I love the taste of victory. Your defeat, of course. Maybe if you weren't so careless, it wouldn't have been so easy to track you."

A tear started to roll down Howard's face. "I'll do whatever you want, Professor Jones. I won't say a word."

"Buck up, kid. It's so unbecoming to see a grown man cry. I won't tell your dear Isabella. Your secret is safe with me." Steve started to smile and took yet another sip of coffee. "I could use another croissant to go. How about it, Howie?"

Howard immediately got up and bought Steve another croissant and returned to the table.

"Aw, thanks champ. You know that it's been great working with you. We should continue to work together. Maybe when you graduate, and you most certainly will with my continued support, we will continue to work together just like we are now. We've got a great thing going. You need my name to publish in top journals."

"Oh yes, yes. I promise that I'll deliver and write solid papers."

"I know you will, Howard. Because if you don't, you know that your perfect little home life will be destroyed." Steve got up from the table, walked behind Howard and leaned into his ear. "Don't mess with me. I can ruin your life. Don't ever forget that."

Howard put his head into his hands and started to weep.

Over the next few months, Howard completed two papers, which were later published in leading academic journals. Howard had shown his cards, and he had underestimated Steve's willingness to get what he wanted.

21

Carlos and Wayne had been working long hours for weeks. They had no leads on the disappearance of Natasha and had spent weeks following Steve. They had not found anything suspicious. Steve was a mundane and regimented person loathed by his students and colleagues. But being a jerk was not illegal.

Carlos had interviewed most of Natasha's friends and co-workers. They had nothing but wonderful things to say about her. She had no enemies, and it was not clear who would want to hurt her. She had no reason to just up and leave. It was not like her, and Carlos knew this. He was convinced something tragic had happened.

Carlos was under serious pressure not only to solve Natasha's case, but also because of the increasing number of dead bodies being found around Miami Dade County. The murder rate was rising steadily, as organized crime continued to be a serious threat to tranquility. Miami had the displeasure of being a drug hub for narcotics coming in from overseas. The Port of Miami was a cesspool of corruption and disorder.

Journalists brought even more stress to Carlos. They were always questioning the Miami Dade Police Department's competence and ability to close cases. News people were rude and demanding, often twisting the detective's words and taking up much of their time, only to use an insignificant quote taken out of context. Families also wanted answers, oftentimes waiting on the steps of the police department to ask questions. Journalists kept publishing stories about the number of missing persons. This led to countless protests. The police commissioner was feeling the heat and constantly beat down the officers for "being lazy". Consequently, Carlos had slept at his desk or his car four out of the last seven nights to make the nagging go away.

Carlos decided to use some of his contacts in the criminal underworld. Carlos and Wayne went to the main jail, located next to the courthouse in downtown Miami, to speak to someone who knew Steve Jones. Carlos often relied on informants to get to the bottom of cases. These "rats", as they were referred to by criminals, sometimes gave good information.

Carlos hated going to the jail. It smelled of body odor and human waste. Silence was a rare commodity, as there was constant yelling. Carlos often wondered how people got any sleep. The answer was simple: there was no such thing as a good night's sleep in jail.

When Carlos walked into the main building, he noticed the walls were wet, the ceiling leaked and had mold growing on it. The jail was falling apart. Clearly, it was underfunded, but it was also overcrowded. On average, twenty-five inmates shared a single cell. The men were bunched up, one on top of the other like sardines. That explained the six stabbings in the last week, up two from the previous week.

Carlos climbed the steps to the second floor of the main jail.

"Look, I just want to know why murders are increasing. Is

there a war going on? If you tell me, I'll get you a nice cold soda like this one right here ..." Wayne had a can of cold pop in his hands. He lifted it to his lips and took a nice long gulp. "Ah, so refreshing."

"Hey man, can I get a sip right quick?" The inmate watched Wayne drink, his eyes sunken into his skull.

Wayne looked at the inmate's white nationalist tattoos and wondered how a person could be so hateful. "You can have an entire can. I've got two more in the fridge. You can have one if you tell me what I need to know."

Meanwhile, Carlos made his way to the main office.

"Good to see you, Carlos," said one of the correction officers. "You look tired. Get some rest."

"Thanks, José. It's been a rough couple of weeks. I'm just trying to close cases."

"Let me know if you want to hit the course one weekend. It's been forever since we played golf. Has your game gotten any better? I'd love nothing more than to take your money."

"I stink. I haven't even been to the driving range in six months."

"We all stink. What brings you here? Who do you need to see?" asked the corrections officer.

"I need to see James Willis. Is he still in protective custody?" asked Carlos.

"Yes, sir. He's in block five. Go on through, Boss. And don't forget my offer. It'd be great to catch up and hit the links. It's been too long."

High-profile inmates or people at risk, like James Willis, were placed in protective custody. James was released after the Supreme Court of Florida granted him a new trial, where he was found innocent. The prosecutor had used a bitemarks expert, which led to James being convicted of the rape and murder of a twenty-year-old college student. In the new trial, the defense council brought in dozens of experts discrediting bitemark analysis and the credentials of the expert used in this case. Dr. Fred Bridges was a former dentist who had become a full-time expert witness and peddled outlandish theories and junk science. Dozens of innocent people were rotting away in prison thanks to the good doctor.

Today, James was sitting in the main jail for driving without a license.

"Willis, you've got a visitor," said one of the correction officers.

"Is it my lawyer?" asked James.

"I'm not your secretary. He's waiting for you. And you must be one dumb S.O.B. to get off after your charges and end up back in here for driving without a license."

Most corrections officers were too busy to know the inmates and what they were charged with. Yet the James Willis case had been in the news every day for months. He could not afford to bond out and was in the county jail for nine months before his case went to trial. Previously, he spent three years in prison before being released after the verdict in his new trial.

Carlos was sitting in the interview room when the guard opened the door and said, "Here he is. Our most famous inmate. It takes a lot to win that honor in this city. Good to see you, Carlos."

"Thanks Officer. Likewise," said Carlos. "Grab a seat, Willis."

"What do you want now? None of you can solve anything on your own. Before I talk, I need to have a few things." stated James.

"We'll get to that in a second, just sit down, and let's have a quick chat," replied Carlos. Naturally, he did not enjoy speaking with James, as he was rude and demanding.

"You know talking to cops in here will get me labeled as a

snitch, right?" James looked around the room and leaned into the table. "They had to put me in protective custody because I was getting beat up all the time when I was in general population, waiting for my case to go to trial. You feel me? I need to get up and out of this bitch before I get poked."

"Relax. Nobody knows you're in here. I wanted to ask about Dr. Steve Jones. He worked on your case for free, right?" Carlos adjusted his tie.

"'Ey, man, let me get a two-piece meal or else take me back to my cell," demanded James.

Carlos had no choice but to send out for fast food. Time ticked away as Carlos waited for the food to arrive. He watched James hungrily wolf down a leg and thigh. James was in heaven as he dipped the meat into the mashed potatoes and shoved it down his throat.

"Easy does it. Slow down, man, you're going to choke. If anyone was to see you eating like that, they may force you to be a Suzie," said Carlos as he laughed for the first time in days.

James finally finished and licked his fingers.

"Finger-licking good indeed," smirked Carlos. "Okay. Back to work, if you would be so kind. Do you know a Dr. Steve Jones? I think he worked on your case, correct?

"Yeah, he did. He's smart, unlike these public defenders. My lawyer thought he could help. He was willing to work for free. That's all I needed to hear."

"What did you think of him?" asked Carlos. He loosened his tie this time. If he looked more relaxed, maybe James would open up more. "He's a person of interest for a case that I'm working on. Nothing more, nothing less. I don't want to let him or anyone in here know that I came here to see you."

"Your secret's safe with me."

"Let's just hope no one offers you any chicken. Just kidding but thank you. Hopefully, nobody connects the dots with you being out here and that delicious smell."

"Yeah, man. I won't say nothing," promised James.

"Good. I wouldn't want to have one of our finest corrections officers start some rumors in here."

"Calm down, Detective. I *won't* say anything. I'm getting up and out of this place soon. Look, I don't keep in touch with Steve. I appreciate him helping me with my case, but he's a real asshole. He just wanted to be in the press. He was using me. We paid him with free publicity. It was just another feather in his cap."

"Did anything seem off about him?" asked Carlos.

"He's a weird dude, man. I didn't like him. If he was up in here, he would get poked on day one. But I'm sure he's not the only law professor who's strange."

"How much time did you spend with him?"

"A fair amount, but less than my other lawyers. I had four lawyers working on my case. Professor Jones was supposed to be our brilliant legal mind who helped with strategies and research." James leaned back in his chair and yawned. "Sorry, man. I got the *itis*. It's impossible to sleep in this bitch. People yell and scream all day and night. As I was saying, he seemed like another arrogant professor who thought he was smarter than everyone."

"Do you think he actually helped your case?" asked Carlos.

"I do. He knew his shit. He also put us in touch with one of the legal academics writing about bitemarks. The guy was from Harvard and waived his twenty-thousand-dollar fee to help me."

Carlos and James spoke for an hour. James confirmed some of what Carlos already knew about Steve's personality, but there was no smoking gun. Carlos had a gut feeling that there was more to Steve than he knew. Yet instincts alone were not enough. He needed hard evidence.

Eventually, Wayne came in to collect Carlos, and they left the main jail in downtown Miami. They then paid visits to the next of kin of several of the other victims. Carlos and Wayne tried to see if Steve was linked to these cases. The family members were still in shock, and there did not appear to be any connections to Steve.

22

STEVE MAINTAINED A LOW PROFILE OVER THE NEXT FEW MONTHS. He managed to exploit his research assistants and publish several more academic articles in leading journals. But beneath his success, there was an urge welling up inside of him. Steve needed to feed his rage. He often called it feeding the demon inside him. He was addicted to anger, and with every perceived slight, he wanted revenge. For this reason, he decided to travel to Fort Lauderdale to pay a visit to Alison Green, the obnoxious mother of one of his former classmates.

Alison Green was a retired physician who studied medicine at Stanford and trained at Harvard. She moved to South Florida and her daughter, Elizabeth, and Steve went to middle school and high school together. Alison and Elizabeth also lived down the street from Steve and his parents. Alison was obese, and so was her husband. He died at the age of fifty of a massive heart attack. Steve used to joke that Alison probably killed him with high-calorie meals.

For no real reason, Alison hated Steve. Every time she saw him walking home from school, she would insult him as well as any of the other children who passed by her house. Steve would purposely avoid walking by Alison's house, as he did not want to run into her watering her garden. Of course, she had the best garden. Dr. Alison Green was the best at everything. If they would have given out Nobel Prizes for ruining people's days, she would have won every year. As a child, Steve never understood why he and the other kids were targeted. He was afraid of her and her massive size.

Allison was rude to every child she came across except her own. Elizabeth, her first daughter, was a straight-A student. Alison would tell anyone who would listen how Elizabeth was going to be a famous doctor. At a parent-teacher meeting, Alison cornered Steve after his short presentation about his possible future in law and said, "If you don't get straight As, it will be tough to make it into the ivy league. It'd be a shame for you to be just another ambulance-chaser. But I wouldn't be surprised."

Steve's mother had just stood there, wishing she could be somewhere else.

But Steve was not the only one Alison tortured. She enjoyed telling young kids that they were not smart enough and would be failures in life. Steve was patient; he had wanted to kill Alison Green for decades. Spring break seemed like the perfect time to do so.

She'd moved to a small home in Fort Lauderdale after her daughter graduated from college, and spent most of her waking hours insulting people on social media. She had thousands of followers for that very purpose. Alison still viewed herself as a leading authority on everything and insisted on telling people how much she knew and how much everyone else did not know.

After four days of watching her, Steve entered Alison's home at 10 on a Thursday night. She was on the computer, typing up a dissertation on why it was so important for government to outlaw soda. Steve crept up behind her and put a rope around her head. He quickly pulled it tight before she could scream. Alison started to squirm and cry.

"What is this? I can't breathe. Please! Stop!" screamed Alison.

"Let's talk for a minute," said Steve. He held the rope in one hand and pulled out his gun with the other hand. "If you scream, I'll blow your brains out. Do you understand, good doctor?"

Alison nodded. The tears started to pour down her cheeks. Her heart beat fast. She thought that she was going to have a heart attack.

"Turn around slowly," said Steve with a grin.

Allison turned around and looked at Steve, puzzled.

"Do I know you?" Alison looked at Steve closely. "Steve? Steve Jones?"

"That's right, Dr. Green. Could you show me all your awards and your degrees? Seriously, I'd love to see them."

"What do you want?"

"What? No 'great to see you, Steve' or no 'hey how're you doing, Steve'? Oh no, that's not your style. Would you like to start our conversation with a quick insult? You can tell me how I'm stupid and was never as good as your daughter."

"Please! What do you want from me?" Alison was crying hysterically.

Steve yanked the rope tighter and put the gun to her head. "I just wanted to pay you a visit and ask how it feels to be such an awful person. I can only imagine how many kids ended up in counseling for years because of you. Not me. I'm a success. You, on the other hand, are still a fat piece of shit."

"I don't know what you're talking about. Please don't hurt me. Do you want money? I can give you jewelry," offered Alison.

"Jewelry? Please. I just want you to apologize. It's that simple."

"For what?"

"For being such a monster, for torturing me every day of my childhood. Do you know how difficult it was for me to grow up? My parents hated me, and so did you."

"I'm sorry. Is that *all* you want? Please let me go."

"You're really the worst person I have ever met. You ruined the self-esteem of so many kids. It's time for you to pay for your sins." Steve grabbed a bottle of Oxycodone pills and forced Alison to take six pills. "Open wide." Steve pointed the gun at her head.

"Please let me go," yelled Alison.

Steve made her write a suicide note before forcing her to hang herself.

Mission accomplished. It felt so good. Well worth the wait.

Steve drove back to Miami, listening to heavy metal music. The adrenaline was coursing through his veins. He could not stop smiling. It felt like the years of abuse had suddenly disappeared. He knew that the cops had stopped following him, and he could get away with another murder.

23

JANE WALKER WOKE UP AT 6 A.M. THE STRESS OF BEING AN
associate dean sometimes caught up with her. At times, Jane
wanted to return to the faculty. While she enjoyed her job,
working with people like Steve made it difficult. Jane knew that
if she could stick it out a few more years, she would have a shot
at becoming dean.

Jane took the morning to read the newspaper and gather
her thoughts. She drank her coffee and listened to classical
music on her beautiful balcony in the suburbs of Coral Gables
before heading off to work. She shook her head. It was a crazy
world, with so much evil. She enjoyed the mornings, but the
brutality of the world kept her anxious.

Jane got dressed and opened the garage to her single-family
home and headed off to work. She spent the day in meeting
after meeting. Steve's name came up at least three times.
Complaints against him were a perpetual drain on her professional life. The university did not know what to do with him.
Steve was even worse than usual after being denied promotion
to full professor. Jane was constrained by university regulations
but was considering trying to change them, a wildly unpopular

move. She did not imagine her life this way but took the associate dean position for the pay raise and status. Yet the proverb rang true: the increment was not worth the excrement.

"I'm off. Ugh, see you tomorrow," Jane said to her assistant after a long day at the office.

"Have a nice night," responded the assistant.

Jane headed to her car in the parking lot. On her way, she received a call about a doctor's appointment later that week. While she spoke, she approached the car and popped the trunk. Jane was not paying attention and threw her briefcase in the trunk. A putrid smell hit her in the face like a tidal wave. She staggered backward and let out a huge groan. Seeing two dead racoons, Jane screamed at the top of her lungs, falling backwards, and scooting away as far as she could. Onlookers rushed to her assistance but there was really nothing to be done. Someone called the campus security. The security guard informed her that they could call the police and file a report. She asked to see the parking lot cameras. The security guard told her that the cameras in the lot were not working.

"It's been such a long day, and now this." Jane wiped beads of sweat forming on her eyebrow. "I just want to go home. I'm not going to waste my time filing a police report."

"Are you sure?" asked the security guard.

"Yes. I'm sure. I know a few people at the law school who are not too happy with me and would do this nonsense. It's not worth my time. I'm busy and have better things to do."

"Understood. Anything else I can do for you?"

"I'll be okay. Thanks, Officer."

"Have a nice day, Professor."

Jane put her face into her hands and asked, "What did I do to deserve this?" She went to get into her car and realized that she had two flat tires. "You've got to be kidding me," she screamed.

Jane sat in the car and waited for forty-five minutes before a tow truck came and helped her repair the tire.

Steve was in his car, far enough away so that Jane could not see him. He could not stop laughing. He would've put the alligator in her car if it hadn't been so difficult. Steve continued to laugh so hard that he began to cry. It was so much fun ruining her day. He should do it more often.

Watching Jane suffer made Steve's day. He drove to Coral Gables, listening to swing music. He skipped as he walked, winking at the people he saw. Finding himself in a bookstore, he grabbed a cappuccino and bought four true-crime best-sellers to celebrate. These books were more than just mere entertainment. He wanted to learn from the mistakes of others and keep honing his craft.

Steve left the bookstore and headed to his apartment. He cooked himself a steak dinner and spent the evening thinking about his next moves. His jovial attitude changed instantaneously into one of somber contemplation. He had plenty of enemies, and Jane was one of them. Sitting alone in his apartment, Steve let his mind run wild, which was a dangerous proposition. He thought of every person who wronged him even in the slightest. This put him in a dark place, and thoughts of murder filled his mind. Most people were idiots. He was so much smarter than those other killers. One person's name kept repeating in his mind: Frank Stanford. And there he sat, stone-faced, until the sun came up again.

24

CARLOS WAS FACING A LOT OF PRESSURE FROM HIS FAMILY TO FIND his niece. Natasha's mother fell into a deep depression and would spend days at home with all the blinds shut. She would lie in bed and cry. Her workload suffered, and her colleagues noticed. Given the severity of her depression and anxiety, her bosses told her to take disability leave.

Carlos witnessed his sister's decline and wanted to solve the crime more than anyone. He still did not understand who would want to harm Natasha. Carlos came up with dozens of different theories about Steve, but he did not have a shred of evidence. These theories revolved around Steve discovering the identity of the anonymous complaint. Yet it seemed that everyone at the university had lodged some complaint against Steve. But Carlos still had this nagging feeling that Steve was involved in more than he let on. Carlos had years of experience under his belt and had a strong sense of intuition.

He spent hours trying to solve the case of the dead divorce attorney. He was able to get ahold of her client list and found out that the attorney was hired by Steve's ex-wife. Carlos thought that this had to be more than just a coincidence. He interviewed at least thirty former clients and friends of the deceased divorce attorney, but nobody had any real connections to Steve. The phrase "no man is an island" did not apply to him.

Carlos wanted to find Steve's ex-wife. He was ecstatic about the prospect of interviewing her, but he soon learned that she had died in a tragic accident. Carlos started calling Steve "Dr. Doom" because everyone around him seemed to end up dead. Yet there was no proof that Steve killed his ex-wife, or anyone for that matter.

The long hours were taking a toll on Carlos. He could not sleep, forgot to eat on time, and spent hours looking through files and records. Carlos wanted to do everything ethically. He prided himself on being the consummate professional and for not succumbing to the tendencies that had plagued the Miami Dade Police Department in the past. Some of his colleagues took unethical and illegal shortcuts to get a conviction, and he and his partner Wayne were not going to go down that path.

After two days, Carlos overheard rumors that local politicians were meeting with members of the police department to discuss the case. Joel Ruiz, the mayor of the City of Miami, met with a local police officer known for bending the rules.

Joel Ruiz was a regular wealthy career politician. He was big with the local Cuban community and catered to their anti-Castro sentiments. Even though Fidel had been dead for some time, Joel knew exactly what to say to get the crowd excited to vote for four more years of nothing. His hair was jet-black and slick, and he wore the finest suits that managed to keep him cool in the Miami heat. He was in good shape for a fifty-year-old, going to the gym several times a week to maintain his self-image of a svelte public figure. He met Ricky Taylor, a cop with a shady past, in the backroom of a local coffee shop in Little Havana. Joel's brother owned the place, and he spent many hours conducting business in the back office.

"Good to see you, Mr. Mayor," said Ricky, the veteran cop. He got up from the table to shake Joel's hand, revealing a fat stomach, his navel peeking out of his shirt to say hello. He smiled. His teeth were yellowing from his cigar habit.

"How's Miami's finest doing? I heard you are up for a Nobel Peace Prize?"

"Maybe in my next life." Ricky had a large grin on his face. "Do you want a coffee and an empanada?"

"Just coffee. How could I turn down the best coffee in town?"

Ricky poured the mayor a shot of Cuban coffee and pulled out a cigar, holding it under his nose and taking a long, labored whiff. "How can I help you, Mr. Mayor?" asked Ricky as he exhaled.

"The media is going nuts over our rising crime rates. I'm going to go bonkers if I read another story about another dead body. I'm facing a lot of pressure from the cops to close the case of the missing law student." Joel massaged his eyebrows with his thumbs and stroked his temples.

"Natasha. She is Detective Carlos Garcia's niece."

"I know. Any leads?"

"It's gone cold," said Ricky as he took a puff of his cigar and leaned back in his chair, yet again exposing his navel to the mayor.

The mayor looked down in disgust.

Ricky noticed but did not care, adding, "Carlos and his partner have been working too hard. They haven't found anything. This girl was an angel. It doesn't make sense."

"What if we find a suspect?" asked Joel. "There're plenty of potential suspects, so arrest someone, alright?"

"The new chief is shaking things up. I don't have the best reputation in the department, as you well know."

"Yeah, sometimes I wonder why I meet you in such a public place," laughed Joel.

Joel and Ricky sat drinking coffee and talking for another hour. Ricky was willing to find a suspect if the price was right. The mayor owed Ricky some favors as he'd helped cover up a driving-under-the-influence charge for Joel's brother three years ago.

"I'll never forget how you helped me with my brother, Ricky."

"Don't mention it. That's what friends are for."

Ricky convinced the mayor to let the case play out a little longer. The nuclear options would be the last resort.

"Carlos is a great detective, Joel. He's by the book. You can't corrupt that guy. He wanted nothing to do with our insurance scam that we were running. The guy says hello, but he doesn't want anything to do with me. He knows that I'm bad news."

"I'll let Mr. Righteous keep working. You better be right on this. We'll be in touch. If I call on you to help me with this, it must be a bulletproof scheme. I don't need another scandal. I've got a chance of running for governor," explained Joel.

"Roger that, Boss."

"I never forget loyal friends. I've got everything planned out." Joel took a long sip of coffee. "I'm going to be governor for four years, and if you want to come with me to Tallahassee, you need to finish up this business. Then, I'll run for president. Heck, even if I lose, I can become a lobbyist and cash in big time."

"Mr. President. I like the ring to it," said Ricky. He took a puff on his cigar. "Heck, I could be the director of the FBI. We're going to run things."

Joel was a political machine. He was willing to break the rules and do whatever was necessary to win at all costs. Joel was a former lightweight boxer, and he viewed politics as a street fight. Nobody could stand in the way of his ambitions. Ricky saw him as his ticket to fame and wealth. If some innocent man had to rot in prison for Joel to stay in power, then so be it.

25

STEVE TRAVELED TO NEW JERSEY FOR A LAW CONFERENCE. HE was supposed to present a working paper that one of his students wrote for him. In typical Steve fashion, he did not thank his co-author. In fact, Steve removed her name from the draft of the paper and presented the work as his own, giving no acknowledgement to anyone.

The conference was held at the College of Central New Jersey, an elite university located in central New Jersey. Steve arrived on Wednesday night and was supposed to present Thursday and Friday. This afforded him the opportunity to explore this beautiful Garden State city. But the conference was not the primary reason for his visit. The academic conference gave Steve the opportunity to seek revenge against Frank Stanford, a leading expert on the economics of crime.

Steve and Frank had attended NYU at the same time, taking several classes together. The two started out as friends but eventually had a falling out. After a simple argument over the legalization of marijuana, the two hated one another. Frank viewed Steve as an insufferable person who constantly interrupted those that he considered less intelligent while taking the time to talk about how smart he was. Frank was more talented at statistics-and-data analysis than Steve. This caused Steve to become extremely jealous of Frank. In class, Frank would pick apart Steve's arguments, using statistics to invalidate Steve's perspective. This left Steve feeling inadequate with an ever-constant feeling of betrayal and revenge dominating his mind.

Steve took the opportunity to badmouth Frank every chance that he had. Before Natasha was killed, she reached out to Frank via email. She told him that she believed that Steve was using one of his ideas and not citing him, which was a mortal sin in academia. Steve used a conceptual typology developed by Frank, but Steve used different words to explain the same argument. Natasha was working on this paper with Steve, and she told him that Dr. Frank Stanford published an article several years ago where he developed the same concept. Steve refused to acknowledge that he was stealing Frank's idea and told Natasha that he would make her life miserable at the law school if she reported him.

Steve received an email from Frank several days after Natasha's email to Frank. The email indicated that it had come to Frank's attention that Steve was submitting a paper where he ripped off Frank's ideas and sold the new conceptual concept as his own. Steve did not tell Natasha that Frank had emailed him. Natasha also asked Frank not to mention that she had reached out to him, but it was quite easy for Steve to deduce that Natasha was the only person who had any knowledge of the paper's contents.

Steve also learned through a friend that worked in another department at the College of Central New Jersey that Frank was trashing Steve among colleagues. He was devising a plan to report Steve's inappropriate behavior. Frank had several meetings with his department chair, a senior scholar in the field, and other academics on what could be done.

Steve had to get rid of Frank before he made things worse.

The conference at the College of Central New Jersey was large enough that Steve could avoid running into Frank. Steve had made three previous weekend trips to New Jersey to find out more about Frank and where he lived. Steve learned that Frank was single and lived with his cat in an apartment located ten minutes from campus.

Steve had a hard time staying focused while at the conference. Listening to the research and opinions of others bored him immensely. He presented his paper and served as a discussant in a panel on juveniles serving life in prison. By the time the panel was over, he felt the need to escape. After the panel, Steve excused himself, needing to get some fresh air.

He walked around the campus, one of the oldest universities in the United States. Even with the darkness surrounding his thoughts, he took the time to admire the architecture and history. He passed a statue of founding father Benjamin Franklin, who once graced the very halls Steve was now in. Steve gazed at the statue, hoping that he would one day be remembered in the same way. He continued walking and happened upon a young couple taking wedding photos. Marriage was for suckers. Remembering his bitch ex-wife, he shook his head, but then chuckled as he remembered her fate.

After a quick bite, Steve went back to his hotel and plotted his attack. After some time, he donned a hoodie and track pants and jogged to Frank's apartment. When he arrived, he noticed there was no car in the driveway and the lights were off. He then looked around and, seeing no one, tried to open the front door. It was open. Wow, what an idiot! He'd forgotten to lock his door. People like Frank were so blessed; they didn't see the world as a dangerous place. He waited for Frank to return home and looked at photo albums. He found a photo of him and Frank sitting together, sharing a beer. Huh, he remembered that day. That's when they used to be friends. Frank should have treated him with the respect he deserved. They could've been a great team.

Frank arrived at his apartment around 10 p.m. Steve was sitting on the couch with a loaded gun.

"Tinkerbell, I'm home. I know you must be hungry." Frank put his coat on the coat rack next to the door. "Tinkerbell? Where are you?"

Frank turned on the lights and saw a man with a ski mask sitting on the couch, a gun pointed straight at him.

"Don't scream. I'll blow your brains out." Steve jumped up from the couch and approached Frank.

"What do you want? Please don't hurt me. I've got a watch and some money in my room."

"Grab a seat on the couch." Steve put the gun to Frank's head. "Great to see you, Frank old buddy. You look good. For now, anyway."

"Do I know you?" asked Frank. He had not spoken to Steve for over a decade. He could not stand Steve in graduate school and tried to avoid him like the plague.

Steve also had the ability to change his voice and spoke with a slight southern accent. "Indeed, you do. We're old friends, pal."

"Please don't kill me, I'll do anything."

Frank sat on the couch as Steve held the gun over his head. Steve took off his mask.

"Steve! You scumbag. Let me go before I call the cops."

Steve took out a knife from his pocket and cut Frank on the cheek. Blood ran down his face, and Frank began to scream.

"If you scream again, I will blow your head off." Steve put his hands around Frank's neck. "You learn a lot about someone when a gun is pointed at their face."

"What do you want?"

"I'm here to seek revenge. A little birdie told me you've been bad-mouthing me."

"No, I haven't. Please."

"Then what's this I hear about me stealing your idea?"

"You can have it, I don't care."

"So, you admit I stole your idea. Do you have proof?"

"Your research assistant emailed me and told me what you did. I was wrong," said Frank.

"I know. You blew her cover. Do you know where she is now?"

"You didn't hurt her, did you?"

Steve walked back and forth, but he never stopped pointing the gun at Frank. "I killed her and fed her to the alligators. The entire Miami Dade Police Department is up in arms and is looking for her. They don't have anything on me."

"You're a murderer?" asked Frank. He started to vomit.

Steve took out his knife and cut Frank's other cheek.

"Stop!"

"I love watching you suffer."

"You're a monster, please, stop!" yelled Frank. He could not stop sweating. "I'm going to pass out."

"The truth is that I love killing people. I killed a random guy the other day at 3 a.m. Just because. No rhyme or reason. He was just in the wrong place at the wrong time. Talk about bad luck! I've killed at least a dozen people just last year. And that was a bad year."

"What do you want? I can take back what I said about you. We can even write a paper together. I'll say it was your idea. Please! I don't want to die, Steve. I'll do anything you want."

Steve forced Frank to write a suicide note. Frank said that he could not handle the pressures of academia and was taking his own life.

"You will never get away with this," said Frank as he looked at the suicide note. He could not stop crying. "The cops will eventually figure out that you did it. I won't tell a soul."

"Nobody will ever know, my dear friend. Do you really think the cops can link me to any of the crimes that I've committed?" Steve paced back and forth like he was giving a lecture to a first-year law class. "Have you ever heard of Israel West? He was a serial killer who crossed state lines. It's much easier for the cops to locate you if you kill in the same radius."

"I'm begging you. I'll give you my retirement account. I'll do whatever you want."

"Retirement? The entire thing? Oh, would you? It's too late. This was a long time coming. You've been humiliating me my entire professional life. Remember our classes? You didn't have to target me." Steve pulled out another gun with a silencer. "What good is your knowledge of statistics now? You are about to become a statistic. Now, take this and shoot yourself. If you don't, I will shoot you, carve you up, and feed you to the wolves."

* * *

Steve had a large smile on his face as he stood over Frank's dead body. Another terrible suicide. Steve spent the next couple of hours cleaning up in the apartment. He had become an expert on crime scenes and could have written a book on getting away with murder. He put out a weeks' worth of cat food before he left, as he did not want Tinkerbell to suffer.

Steve headed back to his hotel. He took a long shower to calm down after the excitement of his most recent conquest. He loved killing and could not get enough.

Steve flew back to Miami Sunday afternoon and kept reliving the kill repeatedly in his head. It would be a week before Frank's body was found. Frank was on sabbatical that year and did not show up to campus regularly.

A neighbor reported a foul smell coming from Frank's

apartment. The building's superintendent went into the room and found his dead body. The superintendent called the police. They searched around and ruled it a suicide, given that there was a gun and a suicide note left on the table.

26

STEVE HAD BEEN LAYING LOW FOR SEVERAL MONTHS IN MIAMI. HE was trying to stay out of the crosshairs of law school administrators. Even Jane was surprised that she had not received a complaint from Steve in a month. Steve was spending his time reading books about criminal profiling, serial killers, and crime scene investigation. He taught his classes with the usual vigor, but the student torturing was kept to a minimum—at least for the interim.

After several months of laying low, Steve felt the urge to kill. He had been tracking his former neighbor, Mitch Ross, a local pain management doctor. Mitch and Steve went to elementary and middle school together. Mitch was bigger and a year older than Steve. He used to beat Steve up at school. During recess, Mitch made it a point to find Steve and inflict pain upon him. Mitch once gave Steve a terrible black eye in physical education class. While they were playing dodgeball, Mitch made it seem that he was avoiding a ball. Jumping left, he elbowed Steve directly in his face. Steve fell to the ground in agony while Mitch backed away, feigning a look of complete shock. The teacher stopped the game and sent Steve to the nurse. Steve remembered that day very well because it left a scar under his right eye.

Mitch had excelled in school and went on to become a doctor. He ran a pain clinic in Miami, which was notorious for pushing addictive painkillers onto desperate people seeking relief. Mitch specialized in getting people hooked on opioids. His business was about volume. In one day, Mitch could see fifty patients and load them up with Oxycodone. He ran an effective pill mill, keeping people hooked on drugs. His office was more like a crack house, with people strung out on opiates, falling over themselves just to get another prescription.

Mitch had been reported to the authorities by the family members of several patients who died from overdoses. The FBI was looking into Mitch's clinic and building a case. Mitch found out that he was under investigation and started using pills to calm his nerves. He was a nervous wreck and planned to escape to Brazil. But he was soon to be visited by a most unwelcome visitor ... who had been thinking about him for many years.

* * *

Steve went to Mitch's million-dollar home in Miami and hid in the bushes. When Mitch stumbled home after a long day of writing prescriptions, Steve jumped into action. He used chloroform to make Mitch unconscious and then lifted the body into Mitch's car. He turned on the car ignition and shut the garage door. This murder needed to be efficient because there was more work to do.

As Mitch's body lay in the car suffering from carbon monoxide poisoning, Steve searched Mitch's home and found a pile of cash under the bed. Mitch had so much money that he did not know what to do with it. There were two million dollars in bags, which Steve promptly gathered up and put into his car.

Mitch's death not only helped Steve feed-the-beast growing

inside him, but it gave him extra money that he could hide in offshore shell companies. Steve had set up fourteen different shell companies and was laundering money. He'd started to stockpile cash in case something happened, or in case he was caught and needed to flee to another country.

Mitch also had several cars outside of his home. Steve pulled his car into one of the other garages and loaded the money into the trunk. He drove off into the night with a big smile on his face. Not only did he have another notch on his belt, but he was also two million dollars richer. Steve had the air conditioning on full blast, as it was a hot and muggy night in Miami. He looked at himself in the rearview mirror. In the dark, he could barely see the scar. It was as if the act of killing Mitch had rid him of his scar. Yet even though he'd killed his former bully, it was clear that the pain of his past was still there.

But Mitch was dead, and Steve had his money. He needed to relax and enjoy the moment.

* * *

When Mitch did not show up for work for three days, one of his employees reported to the police that he was missing. The police found the car still on when they arrived at his home.

Carlos and Wayne were called to the crime scene.

"Carlos and Wayne! How's it going?" asked one of the officers on the scene.

"What do we have here?" asked Carlos.

"Seems to be a suicide. This guy is a local doctor. He's a big player in the pain management world, if you catch my drift."

"Name?" asked Wayne.

"Mitch Ross."

"I've heard about him. The feds have been investigating this guy. Apparently, he writes the prescriptions before the patients can even sit down," responded Carlos.

"Look at this place. Pills must pay the bills. He's got three hundred thousand dollars in cars in the driveway," said Wayne.

"Doesn't look like any foul play. I bet the stress of a lengthy prison term and financial ruin got to him," added the officer.

Carlos and Wayne looked around the house for an hour. There did not appear to be any foul play, as Steve was a master at cleaning up crime scenes. It was clear: the pill boss killed himself. Before Carlos and Wayne headed out, Ricky Taylor, the corrupt cop, showed up at the crime scene.

"My main man, Carlos. How's it going?" asked Ricky, scratching his crotch. Ricky was wearing gray track pants and an old blue sweatshirt.

"It's going. We're just trying to close cases. You know how it is."

"Listen, I want to talk to you for a minute," said Ricky.

"Give me a second, Wayne," said Carlos. He walked to the front of Ricky's car.

"How's the case with Natasha coming along?" Ricky asked, leaning into the vehicle. "I know the department's under a lot of pressure."

"We're at a dead end. We're working like crazy trying to get to the bottom of this. It's been a real grind. To be honest, we're exhausted."

"You know I've got contacts in the government. Maybe I can help you."

"We're all good. Thanks, though," said Carlos with a fleeting smile.

"Let me know. I'd like to help you if I can," responded Ricky.

"Thanks, Slick Rick. I'll keep that in mind. I've got to run. I'll see you around."

Carlos knew what Ricky was implying, and he did not want to get involved with Ricky. For Carlos, Ricky represented every-thing that was wrong with policing. He was corrupt and was not afraid to break the rules or put an innocent person behind bars to solve a case.

Carlos got into the car and said, "Sorry about that, Wayne."

"No worries," responded Wayne. "I was reading the local news. So depressing. It's like all the murderers got together and decided that this would be the week. They think, hey, we can overwhelm the cops, and then none of us will get caught."

"Stay away from Ricky Taylor. That guy is a snake. He wanted to see if there was anything that he could do to help with Natasha's case. He's corrupt. Lots of issues with that guy."

"He's a snappy dresser and seems like a nice enough guy, heh," said Wayne, looking at himself in the side mirror.

"That guy is connected to every corrupt politician and criminal in this city. He just wants to help his friends in high places close the case." Carlos turned up the air and wiped the sweat beading down from his eyebrow. "Wayne, we've got nothing if we don't have our integrity. Guys like Ricky give cops a bad name."

"You got that right; that's what my daddy taught me."

Carlos drove back to the station, where a mountain of paperwork was waiting for him. He needed to complete several pending reports. It was going to be a long night. This was the worst part of the job. There was clearly no rest for the wicked.

27

STEVE SPENT HOURS FOLLOWING THE ASSOCIATE DEAN. HE HATED for Jane to keep advancing in her career. Steve spent several nights camped out at her home, focusing on how he could plot revenge. He memorized her habits, and it was easy; Jane was big into routines. She read a book for thirty minutes to an hour before going to sleep. She often read romance novels, as she needed to unwind from the stress of her university job.

Jane returned home from work the next day at 6 p.m. She opened the door of her home and found a seven-foot alligator in her kitchen. She panicked and ran out of the house as the alligator hissed and thrashed its tail. Steve had contemplated killing the alligator and leaving its dead body in her bathroom. However, he admired alligators too much to harm them. Trapping the alligator was not so easy. Steve paid a local trapper a thousand dollars to catch the gator and keep his mouth shut. The trapper had dozens of exotic animals in his home and had been arrested in the past for killing endangered species.

Jane was pacing around her front yard frantically. Forty-five minutes after her 911 call, the police and animal control showed up. The trapper removed the alligator and told Jane that there was no physical damage done to her home. The kitchen was covered in mud, but it was nothing that could not be cleaned up.

Jane was sweating profusely. Her heart continued to race long after the police left with the alligator. She wanted to file a report. The cops asked if she had any suspects. She said that it was likely a student or faculty member who wanted to get back at her. That list was long given her position, but there was certainly someone on her mind: Steve. She told the police how this was not the first time this type of incident had occurred, recalling the dead racoons and flat tires. Yet when the officer asked Jane to give any names of potential suspects, she kept quiet. Steve had been flying under the radar at the university and things were going well. She worried that the police may question Steve, which could lead to a resurgence of Steve's wrath.

"Is there anything else that we can do for you, ma'am?" asked the officer.

"No. I don't think so. I just don't understand why this keeps happening to me?"

"Are you sure that you don't have any names of potential suspects?"

"I'm a university administrator. I'm sure half the faculty hates me as well as the student body," said Jane with a shrug.

"Don't hesitate to call us back if you need something." He got into his police cruiser and headed off.

Why did this keep happening to her? She couldn't handle it. Jane put her head into her hands and started to cry. Her home was her private sanctuary where she could relax. She felt violated. The fact that someone decided to enter her house while she was gone and put a giant alligator in her kitchen created unprecedented anxiety in her mind. It was like someone wanted her dead.

Jane went back inside and started to clean the mud off the

floor. She vowed to get security cameras and be better about turning on her alarm system. She lived in a safe neighborhood, and nothing had ever happened. Thus, she did not always turn on the alarm. She cursed herself for being so naïve. She scrubbed away, with thoughts running through her mind. Finishing around 2 a.m., she realized she'd had nothing to eat the entire time. She was exhausted. And having little energy to prepare anything, she went to bed, crying herself to sleep.

* * *

Steve was parked down the street out of sight. He turned on his car and sped away. It gave him so much joy watching Jane suffer. He contemplated not being around the crime scene, as he did not want to take any risks. Yet Steve could not help himself. The thrill of revenge always won out, and Steve knew the mission was successful. In his eyes, Jane was pure evil and needed to be dealt with accordingly. His righteous revenge restored order, and he would soon neutralize the threat for good.

Steve turned on some heavy metal music as he drove down the streets of South Miami. He gripped the steering wheel tight and started to yell, "Take that Jane! Don't mess with me ever again. You'll regret the day you messed with me." He punched the roof of his car and screamed at the top of his lungs.

28

CARLOS RAN INTO THE BATHROOM AND BEGAN TO DRY HEAVE INTO the toilet. The disappearance of his niece Natasha and the stress of the investigation placed an enormous burden on his soul. His twin sister's health was also beginning to suffer. Carlos had to check her into the psych ward. Carlos could no longer take the pain of it all. Chief Vargas was right: he was too close to the situation. He slumped over, breathing heavily and began to sob quietly into his hands. He went to bed, knowing that sleep would be brief and unsatisfactory. Why would it be different from any other night that week? His eyes closed and prayed for sleep.

Wayne also saw a change in Carlos' body weight but did not mention it. He knew his partner was in pain. He almost went to the chief but decided against it. He knew that Carlos wanted to be on this case and, as his partner, Wayne wanted to give him support. Wayne wrestled with his thoughts as he wandered around Coconut Grove. The lights seemed to change and when he looked up, he realized he was in the rough part of town. Miami was divided between extremely wealthy and extremely poor places. This area was known for drugs and crime. A few years back, a German tourist found his way into this neighborhood, and his body was discovered the next day.

Wayne turned around, trying to get out of there fast, but it was too late. A group of teenagers was already following him. Wayne stopped in his tracks. He watched the group approach. Some were on small bikes and began to ride around Wayne.

"'Ey, Trey, check out the cowboy," one of the men said.

Wayne sometimes wondered why he wore that hat in Miami, as people always gave him such grief.

"What you're doing here?" sneered one teenager.

"I was just on my way home," replied Wayne. He had a gun strapped to his ankle but did not feel threatened just yet.

"'Ey, man, can you spot me a twenty right quick?" asked another teenager.

"Yeah, man, but I need forty," said another one.

Wayne realized he was in for a rough night. "Sure, I keep it in my sock," he said with a smirk. As a hunter, he appreciated the odds. He bent over and fiddled with his sock until he pulled out a beretta.

"Oh snap, he got a gat!" cried one of the teens.

"Don't pull it out unless you gonna use it," said another, pulling out his own gun.

Wayne fired a shot into the teen's arm, disabling him. The gun clattered loudly on the sidewalk. Wayne then turned the gun on the other kids, but they were long gone. Wayne took the crying teen in his arms and carried him to his car. It was only a flesh wound, and it looked like the gun just missed the bone. As a hunter, Wayne recognized that he would be alright. Wayne took the kid home and patched him up in a small kitchen next to the kid's bedroom.

Wayne didn't say much, just applied iodine and bandages. "You're gonna be alright, kid. Just a flesh wound. I was shot once. My friend shot me in the arm after a shot of tequila before a hunt. Smart, huh. Can you believe that?"

"Ey man! You shot me," said the kid after a period of prolonged silence.

"What's your name?" Wayne totally ignored the comment.

"My skreet name is Big Pudd."

"Yeah? I'm not calling you that. What's your actual name? The name your mom gave you?"

"Paul."

"You almost died today, but you'll be alright, Paul." Wayne felt sorry for him. He was probably just a product of his surroundings.

"What's your name?" asked Paul.

"Wayne, like John Wayne. You know the famous cowboy actor?"

"Naw, I don't watch that."

"What? Cowboy movies are great. Sometimes, they must take the law into their own hands to make sure justice is done."

"Yeah well, we take care of these skreets. The police don't come around here no more, that's why I carry a gun. I pulled mine out before you pulled yours."

Wayne immediately felt guilty but realized he'd had no choice but to equalize the situation. "Anyway, I'll make you a sandwich and call you a cab."

A sandwich was a crappy peace offering, but Paul's face quickly softened and he began to sob. Wayne, who was not very good in these situations, said the only thing that came to his mind: "Want some water?"

"It's so hard out here," sobbed Paul.

"Yeah, I know."

"No, you don't know! My sister was killed a few days ago! I'm trying to stay strong, but I want that guy dead. I know who he is. I saw him. He shot her in her own bedroom, and he ran out. I've got to get him!"

"If you know who he is, just tell the police," stated a bewildered Wayne.

"Nah, man. We don't talk to no police!" screeched Paul.

"Well, you are talking to one now. What do you think about that?"

"Wha ...? Naw man, naw. No way you ain't no police."

The triple negative confused Wayne, but he understood the context of the situation, having grown up in Mississippi. He stood silent, then went over to his jacket and produced a badge.

"Well, aren't you gonna lock me up?" Paul asked, standing up with a look of defiance even as he winced in pain, tears running down his cheeks.

"No. I never wanted this to happen, and I don't think you did either. Let's forget it. You'll be fine. Try to find some new friends and stay out of prison. Just let the police know who did it. Don't throw your life away."

"You don't know how it is out here with your cowboy hat," replied Paul.

Wayne responded by quietly going to the kitchen to make that sandwich.

29

AFTER PAUL LEFT, WAYNE CRACKED OPEN A BEER AND SAT ON HIS couch. It was almost 4 a.m. now, and he could not sleep after all the excitement. He quickly downed the drink and let out a huge belch, rocking his apartment. Feeling satisfied and more relaxed, he spread out on his couch and closed his eyes.

Carlos struggled off the floor of his bathroom and went to bed. He had weeks of fitful sleep, waking up at 3 a.m., his body tense and sore. He knew he had to do something before it killed him. For some reason, he felt the need to text Wayne. He reached for his cell phone and typed a short message: Are you awake?

Wayne's cell phone vibrated, and his eyes popped open. He usually kept his phone far away, so he didn't wake up. Yet tonight was different. Instead of texting a reply, Wayne called.

"Hey, Wayne. Thanks for calling,"

"What's up, Carlos? It's like four in the morning. Everything alright?"

"I can't take this anymore. We need to do something different. You know, Natasha's case? We need to do something drastic. The only thing connecting all these murders is Steve."

"Yeah? What do you want to do?"

"Meet me at the Banana Hammock Club on South Beach."

"On my way," Wayne told him.

* * *

The two drove down to the South Beach area. It was a little after 4 a.m., but the place was lively. Banana Hammock was a loud bar, so Carlos and Wayne could talk freely even though they would stick out like sore thumbs. But that did not matter.

Carlos and Wayne made their way to two open bar stools. People were dancing and having fun. Carlos wished he could be happy like that again. He wished the weight of the world could be lifted, if only for a second. They sat down.

"Alright, Carlos, what's this about? What do you propose?"

"Hey, boys, what will you have?" interrupted the bartender.

"Two beers ... surprise me," said Carlos. After the bartender left, Carlos turned to Wayne and said, "We need to do something drastic. Steve knows the law. He is familiar with how police collect evidence. Every crime scene is immaculately clean, and a suicide note is left at the scene. It's like a formula, and every time we try to talk to Steve, he stonewalls us. No one knows anything. The only thing we have to go on is that somehow, Steve is at the center of all of this."

"Here you go! Two beers all the way from May-hee-goo!" screamed the bartender with delight. "That'll be fifty dollars, please and thank you, or do you want to open a tab?"

"Fifty dollars? For two beers?" asked Wayne, wide-eyed. Wayne never spent any time in South Beach, as he hated the club scene.

"This is South Beach, baby boy," replied the bartender, almost happy to deliver the news to the two beat-up guys who did not belong even on the outskirts of this town.

"Here," said Carlos, handing over a fifty and two dollar bills as a tip.

"Thanks, Boss!" said the bartender as he scurried off. He looked like he did not care. The music and lights seem to energize him.

Wayne and Carlos began to reconsider their life choices, as the police life was not what they had imagined.

Carlos spoke first. "Anyways, like I was saying, we need to do something different. I want to start by searching Steve's house."

"You know that's illegal. We could lose our jobs," Wayne replied, stunned.

"Yes, but what choice do we have?"

"Wait a minute, wait a minute, I need to think." Wayne was not used to the prospect of going beyond the law. He reflected on Paul, the kid he'd shot that night. He thought about how Paul and his friends didn't trust the police and didn't rely on them for justice. Taking matters into one's own hands might be warranted on some occasions.

Wayne took a big, long drink. "Look. If we do this, we've got to realize we could lose our jobs. If Steve is the killer, we could end up dead. We need to be smart about this. Where do we even begin?"

30

STEVE LOOKED DOWN ONTO THE STREETS FROM THE WINDOW IN his apartment and saw a woman walking in the blistering sun. She was tall and well-dressed, wearing a light blue business suit. Something about her hair and clothes made him think about his mother. He remembered that day his mother came home to find him coloring. Steve used to love to color, always keeping in the lines and using colors that would reflect reality. His mother was irritable, muttering to herself. Watching her pour a glass of wine, he decided to give her the page he was coloring.

"Hey, Mommy. Here you go, I did this for you," Steve said with a smile.

She looked at it and didn't say a word. She placed it on the fridge without a glimmer of happiness.

His stomach rumbled loudly. There was usually nothing in the fridge, and today it housed only condiments and apple juice. "What's for dinner?" asked Steve.

"Why do you always ask me that?"

Steve stood silent. He remembered never knowing how to respond to questions from his mother. He walked away and eventually went to bed hungry. This was a common occurrence. As an only child, Steve was lonely. He was left at home for hours on end. This, combined with neglect, made Steve into a very hateful person. He also became spiteful. He began to urinate into wine bottles to get back at his parents, who were too busy trying to be important defense attorneys to pay any attention to Steve. Doing that made him feel good. His parents never noticed, just like they never noticed him.

During his many days alone, he would adventure outside to find squirrels and chipmunks. He wanted to keep one as a pet. One day, he successfully caught a squirrel. The squirrel bit him, but instead of letting it go, Steve twisted his head clean off. He taught that squirrel a lesson, and that made him feel powerful. That feeling of power was addictive. Since he was in pain, he was going to make others feel that same pain.

He began to play pranks on his parents. He would grease the edge of the toilet so that his mother would slide off and bump her head on the toilet bowl. He put dog crap in the mailbox so when his dad went to check the mail, he would get a handful of it. Usually, Steve's parents never caught on, but when they did, he got an alcohol-fueled beating. This made Steve angrier and even more hate-filled.

Steve did not fit in at school, either. He was bullied and ostracized by classmates like Elizabeth and Allison. There was nothing or no one good in his life, just abuse and hate, which he took out on his parents and little animals. Steve soon understood that the answer would be to work hard and go to college. If he could make it to college, he would leave his neighborhood and the people who hated him. He could start over. However, he could not change the person he had become.

Before leaving university, Steve committed his first murder. Steve would walk home from school, across the train tracks. A few steps before the tracks, a panhandler would always approach him and ask for money, shoving a dirty Styrofoam cup into his face. One day the panhandler got a bit aggressive. Steve pushed him away, but he kept grabbing at his bag. Eventually, Steve pushed the panhandler down to the ground. The panhandler hit his head on the track and groaned in pain.

Hearing that made Steve feel good, so he got on top of the man and forcibly hit his head on the track. He did it again and again and again. The clanging sound was loud, but the man's groans were louder. Eventually, the clanging was the only noise. Steve finally came to his senses. He stood up suddenly and looked down at what he had done. Steve looked around and realized he was totally alone.

Backing away from the body, his stride quickened into a jog and then a sprint. He was scared, but inside he had a profound feeling of empowerment for the first time in his life. Steve knew what he did was wrong but discovered a source of strength in his weakness. He sprinted home and up the stairs, saying nothing to his parents. Steve went to the bathroom and threw up into the toilet. Looking at himself in the mirror, he saw someone qualitatively different. He had killed someone. Steve wondered why he would take pleasure in such evil. He felt in control for once. With that admission, he washed up, did his homework, fixed himself whatever he could for dinner, and went to bed.

31

CARLOS AND WAYNE WAITED UNTIL STEVE LEFT HIS APARTMENT to teach his classes. He would be gone for at least five hours. As they watched Steve enter his car and drive off, they knew this was their Rubicon moment: the point of no return. They would be breaking the law. They were both nervous; Wayne bit his fingernails and Carlos's foot tapped on the pedal and the car.

"Should we go now?" asked Wayne, mid-bite.

"No, not yet. We should wait until his class begins in about twenty minutes. He might have forgotten something."

Twenty minutes felt like an eternity. Carlos's stomach rumbled. He had not eaten anything since the morning. This was a huge step in the wrong direction, and he knew it. He was bringing Wayne into it. If things went south, he knew he would not be able to forgive himself. But something had to be done.

Wayne looked at his partner. Carlos was always strong and smart. Yet this case was breaking him. The right thing to do was to get Chief Vargas to take Carlos off the case. It was that simple, yet Wayne could not bring himself to do it. Instead, he was choosing to take his chances on breaking Article 4 of the U.S. Constitution, which protected people from unreasonable searches and seizures. He could not bring himself to act according to the law. Wayne was acting against his own nature for his friend.

"Alright. Let's go." Carlos waved his hands. "Where're those hats?"

In the backseat were two sunhats: one blue, the other white. Everyone wore sunhats in South Florida; not only would they help the two men blend in, but the hats would also hide their faces.

They crossed the street and waited a few feet from the apartment door. A young woman and her puppy walked outside. Putting on his best charming smile, Carlos held the door and he and Wayne walked in. They took the stairs to avoid any elevator cameras, putting on plastic gloves as they climbed. Eventually, they made it to Steve's apartment. Wayne took a credit card and started to slide it up and down to get the lock open. After a minute, it was time for Plan B. Carlos took out a woman's hairpin and started to pick the keyhole. After what seemed like an eternity, the door opened. Luckily, no one stumbled upon their misdeeds.

Carlos and Wayne promptly parted ways upon entry into the apartment. Carlos took the bedroom and Wayne went to the living room and kitchen. Wayne was about to start with the kitchen when he noticed something on a shelf in the living room. Amid books and knickknacks, he saw an oddly placed teddy bear in the middle of the top shelf. It was odd for a man to have a teddy bear, especially one as cold and malicious as Steve. It just did not fit the profile. Moving closer to the toy, Wayne fixed his gaze on the strange object.

While Wayne's attention was diverted from his task of searching the kitchen, Carlos looked under the mattress and bed and found nothing. The closet had a few suits, shoes, and other clothes, but nothing out of the ordinary. Steve had no furniture other than the bed, so he turned into the bathroom.

While Carlos walked into the bathroom, he heard Wayne gasp loudly in the living room followed by an expletive.

"Did you find something?" asked Carlos.

"We've got to get out of here. We're on video. We're being recorded," Wayne shouted in a panic.

Carlos' heart leaped into this throat. He felt dizzy and started to sweat profusely. This was the last thing he wanted. Wayne was fully on camera, and he may have taped himself. Maybe the hats obfuscated their faces? Maybe the camera was not on? Who knows? They both left the apartment, ran down the stairs and exited the apartment complex, pushing the same young woman with her puppy aside. They ran back to their car and sat in silence; only the sound of panting could be heard. Their careers could be over. They could go to prison. Being police officers, they could die in prison.

Carlos eventually broke the silence. "I didn't know this would happen. I'm so sorry."

"It's okay. I did this willingly. Let's just hope for the best." Wayne tried to reassure his partner. He was clearer headed about the situation. "Maybe the camera wasn't recording. Or maybe the quality will be poor? He saw me, but he might not have seen you."

Upon hearing the last sentence, Carlos felt such guilt and shame. Not only was his family in ruins, but his stupid idea could have destroyed his partner's career. He broke down in tears.

Wayne threw his sunhat on the floor of the car and punched the roof. As usual, he was at a loss for words. He said the first thing that came to his mind. "Ah, screw it. Let's get a drink."

32

As Steve drove to campus, he could not shake the feeling that something was wrong. Yet nothing was out of the ordinary. Just a regular day. His cell phone vibrated in his pants pocket but as he was about to check it, a young student wearing a hoodie over his eyes approached him.

"Yo, Dr. Jones, what's poppin, mang?"

"You are not in any of my classes, 'mang,'" replied Steve mockingly. "Who are ...?"

Just as Steve was replying, the student got up close to Steve and stabbed him violently in the stomach. The knife went into his side, four times in quick succession like a jackhammer. The student walked quickly down the hall, dropped the knife, and exited into the stairwell. Steve turned around, confused as to what happened. He looked at the knife on the ground. It was a pocketknife, about six inches in length. He looked down at his stomach. His hand was holding the wound. His pearl-white shirt was quickly turning crimson red. Steve began to feel light-headed as he realized he had just been stabbed by an unknown assailant. Steve fell to his knees.

"I've been stabbed. Help," Steve uttered. He wanted to

shout, but his words came out like a whimper. He leaned against the wall, his eyes seeing posters advertising some political science class. There was a picture of Uncle Sam on a poster that read: We Want You. There was a caption about joining a course titled "Introduction to Security Studies".

Steve chuckled. Great, he got to die in a hall under a poster of some peon prof who couldn't even fill his classes. Steve's vision narrowed; he heard muffled voices. There were people. Then it went dark.

33

RAMON, WHOSE STREET NAME WAS CHELA, WALKED QUICKLY
down the stairs of the university. All he could think about was
the payday he would soon get for stabbing that professor.
Ramon had no ill will toward Steve, as he did not even know
Steve. It was just a job.

Ramon wanted to become a member of a Calle Ocho gang,
a street gang that operated in Miami. The gang primarily sold
drugs but was pushed out by the much stronger Mexican
cartels. As a result, Cuban gangs turned into hired hitmen and
gunrunners. This hit was a chance to join the gang. He could
"make his bones" and become a member, following in his older
brother's footsteps, who'd died in a knife fight with a gang from
Coconut Grove.

Ramon hastened across the university lawn. A car was
waiting for him. His adrenaline was pumping. He jumped into
the car, and they sped off.

"Chela, so did you do it?" asked the driver, who was nick-
named Pepi.

"Yeah, yeah, yeah. I got him good," replied Ramon.

"This will get you in." Pepi was supportive of his friend. He brought him into the life.

They drove in silence as Ramon rocked back and forth. He was excited but knew he needed to calm down. They finally got back to Calle Ocho and walked to a small house three blocks away. Inside was a shot-caller named Tigre.

"Yo, Tigre, Chela did it," said Pepi.

Tigre was slightly obese, but he wore loose-fitting clothes. His eyes were frighteningly beady, with a tattoo of a star just over his right eye.

"Did you see him do it?"

"No, but he said he did," replied Pepi, looking at the floor.

"So, how do you know he did it?" pressed Tigre.

"I did," declared Ramon, speaking out of turn.

"We'll find out. If you did it, you'll get jumped. If you didn't, you'll get jumped but you can take your stupid *culo* home," said Tigre with a smile, revealing his canine tooth.

Pepi and Ramon were silent. They watched Tigre pick up a cell phone. He dialed a number and waited. "Yo, it's done. Tell that punk we're waiting for the rest of it."

The three waited for five minutes until there was a knock at the door. Tigre motioned for Pepi to answer the door. Pepi walked over and opened the door, revealing a young man in T-shirt and sweatpants, his eyes as wide as saucers. It was Howard, the PhD student whose affair Steve had discovered. He was carrying a paper bag and handed it to Tigre. Pepi then snatched the bag and counted the money. He nodded to Tigre.

"That's it then," the young man said.

"No, it's not it," said Tigre. "We said fifteen."

"No, no, I can't manage that. We had a deal: ten thousand dollars."

"Naw. Naw. Naw. We don't have no deal. We said it was fifteen, not ten. If you don't, we'll tell Isabella what's good, kid. We know where you live, remember?"

Howard was shocked. He thought hiring the gang to kill

JONATHAN D. ROSEN & AMIN NASSER

Steve would be the best way to hide his affair. Being black-mailed brought anxiety and depression into his life. He thought about kicking Steve off his dissertation committee, but he feared the repercussions. Howard broke off his relationship with his mistress and focused on his wife. But the feeling of guilt and shame, combined with the fear of losing it all, pushed Howard to make an extreme decision.

His neighbor Pepi brokered the whole deal. Howard and Pepi were friends, but Howard thought Pepi worked at a restaurant. One night, Howard broke down to Pepi, and Pepi said he knew how to fix everything. Howard thought it would all be over and done with, but now he was indebted to a violent street gang.

Howard walked away, worried about his new debt. He hoped that after he paid the five thousand dollars, it would all be over. He could sell some of his father's baseball cards, which was something he hated to do. Yet at least one problem was eliminated: Steve was dead. Howard and his fellow student lackeys would still get their writing credit, but they no longer had to put up with that insufferable man. He ran home, hoping to work up a sweat.

His wife Isabella was at home, waiting for him as she usually did. He walked up to his apartment, and she kissed him tenderly. Howard felt enormous guilt and promised he would never cheat on her again. If he paid off his debt, he would live happily ever after. They slowly made their way inside their tiny one-bedroom apartment.

34

CARLOS AND WAYNE ORDERED ANOTHER BEER. IF THEY WERE
going to go to prison, they would at least go plastered. They
ordered round after round at Third Base, which was their
favorite bar. It was a college bar, so drinks were cheap. The
place was usually flooded in the evenings with college girls and
guys, but it was 11 a.m. The two officers were alone and having a
blast. By 1 p.m., they were surrounded by beer bottles and shot
glasses. Some people came in and left, but it was just the two
officers. They joked about life and relationships, and shared
stories about working at the police department.

"Just what I needed," said Carlos. For the interim, he forgot
who he was and what he was running from. But that was just
what he needed: the chance to forget for a while. That moment
refreshed you. It reminded you that everything was going to
work out somehow because you did your best.

Wayne looked at his partner. He had a lot of respect for
Carlos. He was glad Carlos was able to forget, even if for a short
span of time. He had his own troubles now. It was only a matter
of time until he went to prison. His life was over. For now,
however, he was going to cut loose.

"What now? What do we do?" asked Wayne.

"We wait," replied Carlos.

"Right, but we still have to figure out this Steve guy."

"Yeah. I figure we need to get something concrete."

Just as Carlos was finishing his sentence, his cell phone began to vibrate. It was Chief Vargas. Carlos let it go to voicemail. He was not in the best state to pick up the phone. After ten seconds, the phone vibrated again indicating a voicemail notification. The phone rang yet again.

"You should probably pick that up," laughed Wayne as he took a long swig.

"It's Chief Vargas. I better go outside," Carlos said with a meditative look. He trotted outside and picked up. "Hello, Chief Vargas?"

"Carlos, Steve Jones is in the hospital. Apparently, he was stabbed by a student."

Carlos stood motionless. Without letting on too much he replied, "Oh, that's horrible. Where is he now?"

"I want both of you on this. Maybe he's connected to some sort of human trafficking ring."

Carlos shuddered at the thought, although he knew better. Chief Vargas gave directions to the hospital where Steve was recovering. He was still unconscious but could be waking up any moment. Carlos wondered if this could be an opportunity to change the circumstances. He finished the call with Chief Vargas and went to collect Wayne. Wayne was in the middle of speaking to a woman.

"Alright Wayne. We've got to roll. Steve is in the hospital; he was just stabbed on the way to his office," announced Carlos as he motioned for the waitress to bring the check.

"What? That's great," exclaimed Wayne loudly.

This shocked the lady who became disgusted with her new friend and let out a loud tsk.

"Uh, what I mean is ..."

"Never mind," Carlos said. He threw four twenties onto the table. "We need to catch a cab. Let's go."

35

STEVE WOKE UP IN THE HOSPITAL WITH TUBES UP HIS NOSE AND IN his arm. He had never been in a hospital before. He looked around for a glass of water. Steve had a perishing thirst, but he had difficulty moving. He tried to speak, but only a whimper came out.

Steve had been stabbed in the stomach, and he was still confused. He never saw that student before, but it was quite possible that he went too far. Steve disregarded the thought. Someone tried to kill him. A foolish student, of all people. His anger began to build. He could still picture the person in his mind. He hatched a plan; not only would he kill that person, he would use the attempted murder to his advantage. Maybe it would help him attain the rank of full professor.

A nurse finally came in. She was young, slim, and quite attractive. "Mr. Jones, how you doing, hun?" she asked.

"Doctor Jones. I want some water," Steve replied.

"Alright Mr. Jones, I'll get you some water," she said as she left the room.

Steve looked around the room. He felt very weak. He knew he would be cooped up for at least a few weeks. He looked around for his cell phone but could not find it. If only that stupid nurse would put on the television or something. What did she expect him to do, just lie there like a lump? Maybe that's what stupid people did all day. He needed his mind entertained.

The nurse finally came in with a cup of water. She put it up to Steve's lips, and he slowly sipped. Steve felt much better after that first drink of water.

"Now, isn't that just great, baby cakes?" asked the nurse with a polite smile.

"What time is it? How'd I get here?" asked Steve.

"The doctor will be with you in a moment. Just relax for now," replied the nurse.

"I want answers now. You know what happened, just spit it out," Steve demanded.

"You've been here since noon, and you were brought by the *amber lamps.*"

"That's ambulance," said Steve with a satisfied, devilish smirk. Provoking people was fun for Steve.

The nurse walked out in a huff. It really did not take much to be nice to a nurse, but Steve wanted to feel powerful after being attacked. He felt vulnerable in a hospital bed, reliant on nurses and doctors. Being hostile was a sort of defense mechanism. It was a weird way to feel safe after a traumatic experience.

Steve wanted his phone. He called the nurse by pressing the alert button. A different nurse came in. She was Hispanic, middle-aged, and of medium build.

"What can I get for you?" she asked.

"Hello, madam. Could you kindly find my cell phone? I'm awfully worried about my parents. I'd like to tell them I'm alright," Steve said with a smile, trying to be as charming as possible. He wanted to be polite to mess with the nurses.

The new nurse went over to the foot of the bed where she

produced Steve's cellphone. She handed it to Steve without saying a word.

"Thank you," said Steve humbly.

Steve started to look through his phone. He had a few emails from students and faculty which he promptly deleted. He could use his stay at the hospital to his advantage and ignore people, but he usually deleted emails anyway. He scrolled past news updates until he came upon an alert from his security system. Steve thought hard, as he did not leave any windows open. Maybe some rats set off the alarm. He opened the video link and to his surprise saw two men walking around the apartment. Steve's jaw fell open as he saw one person approach and pick up the camera disguised as a teddy bear. Seemed like the intruder was an expert. Was it another crazy student? No way. He watched as the two men exited quickly. Steve placed the phone down. He felt violated. Not only had he almost died today, now he was being robbed.

36

Carlos and Wayne paid the cab driver. Luckily, traffic was light. Carlos and Wayne raced to the front desk, flashed their badges, and demanded Steve's room number. Carlos and Wayne then trotted over to Steve's room in Intensive Care. Wayne and Carlos both breathed deeply. The detectives stood silent, trying to slow their breathing before opening the door. They wanted to portray tranquility and calm before entering. Finally, Wayne opened the door. Carlos entered first.

"Steve, it's Carlos and Wayne from the Miami Police Department," Carlos introduced them.

A fanged smile curled Steve's lips. He recognized Wayne from the security camera. It was all coming together. Steve knew they were on to him, but he had proof of their misdeeds.

"Officers. How's it going? I never forget a face," said Steve as he looked at the officers, focusing on Wayne.

Wayne felt a shiver go down his spine. Steve's smile and demeanor creeped him out. It was only 2 p.m. and all the fun and alcohol suddenly left his body and mind.

"Yes, well, we're here to discuss your incident today. You

were stabbed on your way to your office," Carlos replied quickly, hoping to shore up his partner's confidence.

"Yes. Yes. Possibly some crazy student of mine, but I never saw him before," Steve replied, still gazing at Wayne.

"Do you think you can give us a description?"

"He was a Hispanic male, about five feet three inches. Medium build. I never saw him before. Nothing really set him apart from other students."

"Did he say anything to you?" asked Wayne, finally feeling confident enough to talk.

Steve smiled and turned to Wayne. "Why yes. He said something like, 'Dr. Jones, what's up' or 'what's popping' or something like that."

Carlos turned to Wayne and said, "We should go back to the university and find out if there's anything on the cameras."

"Yes, cameras can be very helpful," interrupted Steve, first gazing at Carlos and then gazing at Wayne. "Especially when identifying criminals. You never know what or *who* might turn up on a security camera."

Wayne's heart began to race. Steve was letting on that he knew. It was so obvious. But at this point, it was best to remain coolheaded.

Wayne responded nonchalantly, "Well, yes, that's what they're for—"

"Steve, we better get going. We need to start our investigation right away. We'll keep in touch," interjected Carlos, perceiving his partner's discomfort.

"I do hope you catch the person. Important people like myself cannot get stabbed in broad daylight. You'd think that living in such an advanced, developed country, there would be police departments that enforce the law. Goodbye, officers," said Steve. He winked at Wayne.

Steve enjoyed torturing Wayne and fed off his discomfort.

Next time he saw him, he was going to kill him. Steve licked his lips in delight. He had a new target, and new targets gave him the motivation to continue.

37

"Woo-oo-oo-oo! You made it," cried Howard as he opened the door to three of his fellow students.

It was 10 p.m. and he and his wife were throwing a house party. The three students, two women and a man, threw some beers at Howard and went into the living room. Everyone had smiles and the energy was through the roof. Some Reggaeton played loudly as partygoers bumped and grinded vulgarly. There was food and drinks everywhere; the carpets looked like they'd been tie-dyed. It was Isabella's birthday, planned many weeks in advance. However, in Howard's mind, it was also a celebration of the death of a tyrant. Dr. Jones was dead. He was finally rid of the source of his stress. Yes, it was his fault. He'd committed adultery and broke the trust of his loving wife. But it was all going to be okay. He promised he would never do it again, but the way his lady friends were dressed and danced, he knew that promise would be broken ... maybe even tonight. One girl in particular caught his eye. She was scantily clad. He approached her and filled her glass with cheap wine. Her name was Erica, and she was a first-year law student.

"Thank you. Great to be here. Where's Isabella?" Erica asked.

"She's somewhere. I'll go find her," replied Howard.

"Oh, yeah. First, let's chat a bit. I like talking to you."

Howard bit his lip. He knew she wanted him. Steve was out of the way, and Isabella would be as well if she continued to drink like she was.

Isabella was in the kitchen having shots with her girlfriends. It was her birthday. She was playing "never have I ever", so every time she did what was requested, she had to take a shot. She had had five in a row and was feeling great. She was Latina, so she loved everything about Miami. Howard was white Anglo-Saxon, and he had his sights set on the northeast where he could rub elbows with the financial titans. There had always been a cultural divide between the couple.

Howard found Isabella and Latinas to be very passionate, while Isabella found Howard dry at times. She went into the living room and began to dance. She was enjoying every minute. Howard was playing host, making sure everyone's glasses were full of whatever they were drinking. This was not a prim-and-proper event, but a down-and-dirty hoedown.

A few hours later, Isabella staggered to her bedroom. Howard was completely trashed, but sober enough to know he would have his chance with Erica. A few minutes later, he went in to check on her and she was passed out.

Howard returned to the living room and made an announcement. "Alright people, alright. The lady of the evening has gone to bed. Everyone out. Thank you for coming, but you know what they say: happy wife, happy life. So, get out. You don't have to go home but you can't stay here."

As people began to shuffle out, he grabbed Erica and pushed her into the kitchen. He was confident no one saw him do this.

Once everyone had left, he rushed back to the kitchen and began to passionately kiss Erica. They made love and fell asleep on the couch; he'd kick Erica out the door once he'd had a few minutes of rest.

38

CARLOS AND WAYNE EXITED STEVE'S ROOM AND WALKED silently until they were outside the hospital.

"He knows, but I think he's just having some fun. He's a sick bastard," said Wayne with a shake of the head.

"Yes, but I think he's not going to report it. At least for now," Carlos replied.

"What do we do?" asked Wayne.

"Find the guy who stabbed Steve."

"Are you kidding? We should focus on the Natasha case."

"Face it, that case is cold for now. We need to work with Steve. I believe the student wanted Steve to die that day. Maybe that will help us erase any recordings ... or possibly buy us some time. Something will open up soon. Steve *will* make a mistake. Right now, we just need to get him back on the street. Maybe this time we can be more proactive and put a tail on him." Carlos knew they needed time.

"Alright. We'll head to the university and check out the cameras."

The two officers went straight to the university and saw the head of security. The team had everything ready for the officers. They watched Ramon being dropped off and picked up at the university. The license plate was visible and, most importantly, even though Ramon's hoodie concealed his face, one frame in two different parts of the tape clearly revealed his eyes, nose, mouth, and a bit of hair.

They viewed the tape of the stabbing. It was clear: Ramon had indeed committed the stabbing. Carlos sent the police department an APB (all-points bulletin) that described Ramon's physical appearance, his crime, and the possibility that he was a disgruntled student that was armed and dangerous. Wayne instructed campus security to try to identify the student. Such a task would certainly take a few days to complete.

After the work was finished, Carlos and Wayne got Chinese food. Even though they had a huge weight on their shoulders, the two men felt motivated. Carlos felt happy for the first time in months. Maybe it was the alcohol. Maybe it was the thrill of the chase (or being chased). Or maybe it was the satisfaction of finding Steve's attacker so quickly. He didn't know. Wayne felt the same way. He wasn't worried about his future. Somehow, this thing would go away.

39

"Ey, bitch ass! You're on TV," Pepi cried out to Ramon.

"Yoo-ooooo," exclaimed Ramon, in complete shock. "They got me on camera! I need a place to hide."

"Get outta here, son. I don't know your dumb ass," shouted Pepi and shoved Ramon out the front door. "I don't need Tigre on my ass after I vouched for you."

"Come on, mang. I need a place to hide. It's too hot out there," cried Ramon. He knew he was on his own now. He had to find a place to hide and fast.

Ramon ran down the block to find his car. It was the same car he'd used in the heist. All the adrenaline after the stabbing made him and Pepi forget to change the license plate. He jumped into it and drove like a bat out of hell down US-1. His plan was to hide out in the Everglades swamp until things cooled down. He might not be able to join the gang—he had a nagging feeling his life was *over*.

Ramon wove through Miami traffic until he could go no further. Traffic piled up, and his paranoia did not help his thought process. The police could be anywhere, looking for him. He needed to get out of there. He refused to wait; he abandoned his car and began to run. After thirty seconds, he heard police sirens. He did not have to turn around; he knew they were for him.

"Freeze. Put your hands in the air," shouted a police officer behind him.

Ramon took a gun out of his back pocket and fired wildly in the direction of the voice. The officers fired back, hitting Ramon twice in the back and once in the leg. Ramon collapsed in a heap. He turned around and thought about the crimes he'd committed. He always hated himself for what he was and what he'd become. He had no home life and gravitated toward street life. It was clear that he had no friends. No gang would want him after his failure and, ultimately, he was looking at forty years in prison.

Ramon put his gun to his head and pulled the trigger.

40

STEVE WAS RECOVERING. RAMON MISSED MOST OF HIS VITAL organs. The knife did manage to perforate parts of his stomach, but the damage was minor. No one from the university visited, but Steve did not care. He preferred to be alone anyway.

Steve spent his days in the hospital, yelling at the nurses and ordering take-out. He emailed one of his assistants to bring a laptop so he could finish a few articles. In his spare time, he was planning to murder Wayne. He was certain the other man in the video was Carlos, but he couldn't be sure. Killing a police officer was going to be a challenge, but he enjoyed the difficulty. He thought of blackmailing Wayne, but the opportunity had to present itself. Steve also entertained himself by thinking about the man who stabbed him. Three days had passed since the stabbing, and Steve felt it was time for him to leave. Doctors wanted him to stay for observation and refused to grant him leave until they were satisfied.

On the fourth day, a nurse entered the room and announced that there were two officers asking to see him.

"Have them come in," ordered Steve. He had a feeling they were here to update them on the case.

Carlos and Wayne entered the room.

"Officer Briggs and Officer Garcia. Nice to see you. Are you taking some time to see your favorite stabbing victim?"

"Steve, I hope you are doing better," said Wayne with no sign of a smile on his face.

"Now that you are here, I think everything is going to be fantastic. Why are you here interrupting my very delicate convalescence?"

"We've got an update on the case," interrupted Carlos. "Is this the man that stabbed you?"

Wayne handed him a mugshot of Ramon.

Steve looked at the picture, covering Ramon's hair and eyes with his hand. "Yes. Without a shadow of a doubt. This is the person who stabbed me. Who was he? Why did he do it? And where is he now?"

"His name is Ramon Gutierrez. He was just some street kid. He has priors for battery and drunk and disorderly. He was affiliated with the Calle Ocho street gang. We do not know exactly why he tried to kill you. He died in a shootout with police. He wasn't a student at the university, nor was he in any way connected to it. We do not have the resources to further investigate the matter, but we do believe it might have been a contract hit. The gang does that sort of work," summarized Carlos.

There was a long pause. Steve was a bit shocked that someone could be after him. Yes, he had managed to piss off many people in his life, but who could it be? "Hmm. I wonder," said Steve, breaking the silence. "It has to be someone who didn't have the guts to do it himself, or herself."

"Yes. We're thinking that, too. Of course, no one will talk to us. No one wants to be seen as a snitch," Wayne added.

"I do believe the phrase 'snitches get stitches' here rings true. Oh well. Good riddance. I must thank the officers for a job well done. Always happy when they clean up the streets, even if they go to prison afterwards. I think it's acceptable to break the law to save it. Isn't that right, Officer Briggs?"

Wayne held his tongue. He knew there was no good response to such a goading remark.

Carlos nodded and stated matter-of-factly, "It's time for us to go. Be sure to let us know if anything develops, or if you feel threatened. Your life may still be in danger."

"Certainly. Thank you again," said Steve, looking down at his phone and waving his hand as if to sweep the officers out of the room.

41

HOWARD WOKE UP WITH SOMEONE PUNCHING HIM IN THE FACE and body. He jumped off the couch and looked up. His eyes were adjusting to the light, and his head was pounding from the alcohol-fueled frenzy of last night. It was Isabella, and she was furious. Still confused, Howard held out his hands to defend himself and realized he was naked. He looked around and saw an equally naked Erica stumbling around for her clothes. Howard understood what was happening: he'd been caught sleeping with Erica.

"How could you?" demanded Isabella angrily.

"I'm sorry, I didn't mean to, it just happened," said Howard weakly.

"I want you out ... I want you gone," cried Isabella as she ran to the bedroom and began to pack Howard's night bag.

Howard sat on the couch. Erica was almost dressed. She wanted nothing more than to get out of the situation. She was accustomed to being cheated on and thought that this was just another one of those weird situations—but this time, *she* was on the other side of the table.

Howard finally got up and went to the bedroom, grabbing

an apron to cover his shame. He wanted to talk to Isabella and explain, but there was really nothing to say. He'd blown it, and now his marriage was over. Without a word, Isabella shoved a bag into Howard's stomach and then pushed him out of the door.

Howard stood outside the apartment. He had to remove the apron and put on his clothes outside. With a deep breath, he began to walk ... to nowhere.

Howard was distraught. He found himself in the town square and walked over to a park bench. There were homeless people all around, but no one bothered him because he looked disheveled and disturbed. Isabella had packed his phone and charger, and he was greeted with a message:

Dear students,

We are happy to update you on the condition of Dr. Steve Jones. He is resting comfortably at the Miami General Hospital. He is expected to make a full recovery in the next few weeks. We expect him to return to classes in the near future. Please keep him in your heartfelt thoughts and prayers.

Sincerely,

Jane Walker, Associate Dean

Howard's heart sank like a stone. Steve was going to live and continue to torment him. He felt like an absolute failure as he looked idly around. Maybe this was his destiny. He should become homeless because nothing mattered now. Just as he thought that he received a text from Isabella: Come home. We need to talk.

Maybe there was a chance to make this right.

42

CHARLES AND WAYNE ENTERED THE POLICE STATION. THEY KNEW they had to act fast. Steve had Wayne on camera, and he was more than happy to let everyone know that he knew.

"We need help trailing Steve. I think we better reach out to someone to help track him," Carlos suggested.

Wayne agreed. They spent the morning asking colleagues for assistance. One after the other, the two officers were turned down. The department was overstretched, and people were overworked. No one wanted to take on a new case. Carlos and Wayne were getting desperate.

"Alright. How about Donovan O'Malley in the Investigative Analysis Unit? He's probably itching to get out of the office and into some field work," suggested Carlos.

"Yes, I know Donovan. He's a good guy—a bit inexperienced and young, not to mention nerdy, needs to hit the gym— but we don't have much choice," agreed Wayne.

The two officers made their way down to the Investigative Analysis Unit. Donovan was at his desk with his head in his hands. As Carlos and Wayne approached, they saw that he was not busy reading; he was asleep.

"Wakey, wakey, hands off snakey," quipped Wayne.

"I'm not sleeping, *you're* sleeping," responded Donovan flatly.

"Bored, are we? We've got a job for you. We need you to track this guy; his name is Steve. I think he's responsible for a number of killings. He's smart as well."

"I've been following the case. Chief Vargas gives us briefings, you know, the ones you guys have been missing for the past week," a grumpy Donovan responded.

"When you're higher up like we are, you'll get to skip those," said Wayne, throwing Donovan's jacket to him. "We'll give you the rundown over some coffee. Looks like you need it."

They gave Donovan a summary of everything except the violation of Steve's Fourth Amendment rights. As far as Carlos and Wayne were concerned, he was on a need-to-know basis, and no one else needed to know.

"So, I basically follow this guy?" Donovan asked. "That's all? Easy, but also boring. What's in it for me? Chief Vargas is already breathing down my neck about my profiling database."

"We'll talk to Vargas and make sure you'll get a promotion. How's that sound?" asked Carlos, agitated.

"It's a start, I guess. Deal." The three shook hands on it. Donovan was going to follow Steve. Little did he know it would cost him his life.

43

STEVE WAS DISCHARGED FROM THE HOSPITAL AFTER SEVERAL DAYS. The doctor gave him a prescription for potential infections and another for pain. Steve decided to keep the pain medication for another purpose. He had a leave of absence from his work for another two weeks, so he decided to do some investigating of his own.

From Officers Carlos and Wayne, he'd learned that Ramon was hired to kill him. It could have been a student or faculty member, maybe even a member of the administration who'd orchestrated it. Steve decided to pay a little visit to Calle Ocho. He drove to a dive bar next to a place where outsiders were not welcome.

Steve was armed with a knife and two guns, one on his hip and another two strapped to his legs. He was not going into this gangland without proper protection. He first opted to visit a local coffee shop and then a bar. At the local bar, he sat and drank a beer, listening to conversations. The conversations were in Spanish, so he had some difficulty understanding. But living in Miami for so long, he picked up certain words.

He learned that there were gang members operating in the

area and that they were open for business. Steve knew it was impossible to get anyone to trust him enough that they'd take him to the gang leader. He had to know someone who could vouch for him. This was going to be difficult for Steve. He had to make it happen and decided to try something.

Steve walked up to a group of Cuban Americans, talking and laughing. They did not seem to notice him at all.

"Excuse me, *amigos*. I need a favor. Someone tried to kill me, and I know it was one of you folks. If you could take me to your leader, that would be mighty helpful."

The gangsters looked at Steve in silence and started to laugh loudly, like it was the first time they'd seen The Three Stooges.

This annoyed Steve greatly, but he knew that his request would be met with derision. He pulled up a chair, an act that shocked the group. They stood in defiance. Steve, not intimidated, said, "Look, I know this is hard for you, but I need to know who arranged to kill me."

The gangsters grabbed Steve by the shirt and threw him to the ground. The last thing Steve saw was one gangster kicking him in the head.

Steve woke up on the floor with the gang members peering over him. He lifted himself up and exited the bar. He remembered the one that kicked him, and that was his new target. Steve hid himself under the neighboring house and waited. After two hours, his man finally left the bar, and Steve crawled out from under the house. *Let the stalking begin.*

Steve followed the man back to a house. As the man fumbled drunkenly for his keys, Steve crept coldly behind him and put a gun into his neck. "Don't move. We just need to have a little talk. Is there anyone in the house?"

"N-n-no. Just me," replied the man.

"Open the door and remain calm. I just need to ask you a few questions. So easy, my boy."

The man opened the door and the two entered the front room.

"Sit down and relax. Can I get you another beer?" asked Steve. The man remained silent, too scared to answer as he made his way to a ratty, old, and peeling leather couch. "I said, you're going to answer my questions. That was a question, no?"

"Y-y-yes."

"Okay, we're getting somewhere. Would you like a beer?" Steve laughed, taking pleasure at the fear he was seeing on the gangster's face.

"No, Papi."

"Papi?" Steve howled with laughter.

The gang member looked around confused.

After a several seconds, Steve calmed down. "Look, I just want to know who hired your people to stab me. Such a simple request."

The man looked around. It was clear Steve was not a cop, so he was not snitching. No one was there to see the gang leader talk to Steve, and there was a gun to his head, so he had no choice. "Word on the skreet is that it was one of your students. Some white guy. He was pissed because you knew he had been banging a student. And he was scared you would tell his wife," explained the man.

"Howard?" Steve asked in absolute disbelief.

"Yeah. Howard. That's the guy."

"Howard? Well played, young man, well played. Too bad for you and your wife, I lived. How much did he pay?"

"Ten, but we made him pay an extra five."

"Ten what? Dollars? What are you working for? Peanuts?"

"Thousand."

"I'm still offended. What am I, chopped liver?"

The man remained silent.

"What's your name?" asked Steve.

"Pepi."

"Well, Pepi. Thank you very much for your wonderful help. Now, there's something I need to do, but I seem to have forgotten. Do you think you can help me out with that?"

"Yeah, yeah. What do you need? I'll do anything," exclaimed Pepi with unbridled enthusiasm.

Steve looked down at him with disgust. "You call yourself a gangster. You must fancy yourself some sort of romantic street soldier. You're just trash, but here's the good news: you can help me clean up the streets." Steve fired a shot into Pepi's head.

Pepi's head flew back and spasmed. He was soon motionless, with his eyes open. A single tear slid down his cheek.

Steve stared at Pepi for a while, emotionless. He wiped his prints from the gun and placed it in Pepi's hand. He then exited the house through the back door, already planning his next move.

44

DONOVAN O'MALLEY OF THE INVESTIGATIVE ANALYSIS UNIT TIED his sneakers and got ready to do some real work. He was bored of office life, falling asleep every so often. He had a long-distance girlfriend in the Philippines named Donna. They'd met in an online chatroom three years ago. He spent many hours talking to Donna when she woke up and during her lunch break. He hoped to save enough money to move there, possibly starting a private security organization. The current administration paid serious money for bringing down drug dealers. The Filipino government's no-tolerance policy was brutal, but it could bring in more money for Donovan than what he currently made. He was ready to go, leaving a message for Donna saying that he would be back in a few hours. His objective was to follow Steve without him finding out. This was a stealth mission.

Donavan went to Steve's house and paid close attention to his movements. Steve had just checked out of the hospital after his stabbing, so Donovan thought it would be an easy assignment. The guy would just be resting. Maybe he'd do some reading and catch up on some work. Donavan opened the bag of beef jerky he'd bought for the stakeout. He liked stakeouts, an excuse to eat he called it. He paired his beef jerky with a large tub of hummus, pita bread, and a hunk of gouda cheese. He liked Chinese food, but today he felt like something healthier. He washed it down with an energy drink.

Donovan ate and watched people walk by. Eighty percent of stakeouts required sitting and watching. The other twenty percent was following and taking notes. Wait for it—there he was! Donovan watched Steve drive away, out of the underground parking garage. Donovan turned the key in the ignition and slowly followed Steve's car, trying to look inconspicuous.

Donavan followed Steve into the Calle Ocho area, where he parked his car. Steve circled the block and parked in the same parking lot. He saw Steve far off and followed him into a rough-looking dive bar. After a few moments outside, pretending to smoke a cigarette, Donavan made his way into the bar, keeping his head down. He went up to the bar, out of Steve's view, but then he saw Steve go over to the table and get beat up.

Donavan was completely puzzled. Why was Steve there? Why was he talking to those people? What did he say to them? What the hell was going on? When he saw Steve exit the bar, he knew he had to follow, so he casually got up. By that time, however, Steve was gone.

Donavan looked around, smacking his cigarette carton for about thirty seconds. Assuming he had missed his chance, Donavan headed for his car, pulled out his cell phone, and called Carlos.

"So?" asked Carlos.

"I lost him. He was at a bar in Calle Ocho for some reason. He said something that I couldn't quite hear, and then he got a beating. He left the bar after that. I followed him, but as soon as I exited the building, I lost him. It's like he vanished into thin air."

"Alright, keep at it. Did he park his car somewhere?" Carlos asked.

"Yes. I'm going to my car. I'll see if his car is still there," replied Donovan.

Returning to his car, Donovan saw that Steve's was still there. Relieved, he sat down and waited. He watched gangsters go back and forth, pants sagging. Steve pulled out his cell phone and saw that Donna messaged him a photo to say good morning. She was just getting ready for work and wanted to show her man her outfit. Donovan smiled. He thought he could easily catch a flight right now and be with her. He could work odd jobs until he made enough money to start his private security business. He began to daydream about life with Donna, waking up next to her instead of a photo of her. Just as he was thinking that very thought, Steve made his way to his car. What was that bastard up to? Where did he go? Why did it take over two hours to get back to his car?

Donovan followed Steve back to his apartment, an altogether uneventful and boring ride. He parked outside the apartment and watched. After a few minutes, a light turned on inside Steve's apartment. Donovan called Carlos back and reported the events. After the call, Donovan went back to his own apartment and waited to call Donna. She told him about her day at work, as Donovan prepared dinner. They spoke late into the night and early morning, planning their future.

45

CARLOS GOT OFF THE PHONE WITH DONOVAN. HE WAS IN THE office catching up with paperwork all afternoon. Wayne sat across from Carlos, picking his nose, not a care in the world. He was distant, thinking about hunting alligators. He preferred the outdoors to sitting in a hot office, waiting for Donovan to report.

Carlos updated Wayne on Steve's movements throughout the evening.

Wayne was puzzled and asked, "Why would he go down there? Do you think he went down to Calle Ocho to find out why some gangster stabbed him?"

Carlos thought hard, rubbing his forehead. "It would make sense. We told him who stabbed him and whom he was affiliated with. He knows," said Carlos and sighed softly.

"We have to get some rest. Let's take the day off tomorrow. Let's go fishing, rustle us up some gator meat." Wayne had a big smile on his face. "It's time for us to take a break, get some fresh ideas. We should keep a tail on Steve; Donovan did an okay job. Anyone could lose a guy."

Carlos agreed. It made no sense to wait around the office.

He wanted to do some fishing. It also made sense to keep a check on his mental and physical health. A day outside would do them both good. Donovan would keep on Steve and report back often. The two officers made plans for the next day and notified Donovan. Things were looking up, as long as they were on the offensive.

46

Upon returning from Calle Ocho, Steve felt a renewed sense of vigor. His head was still throbbing after the painful beatdown he'd received from the gang. He wondered what might happen once they discovered that Pepi was dead. The gang would be missing one of their members. Maybe they would come searching for him. Maybe those hoodlums wouldn't be able to put two and two together. No. Steve had just wanted to talk, and that's all they knew.

Steve turned the TV on and hoped for a news story on increased gang violence in the Miami area. He prepared dinner and sat down to answer or delete emails. He was due back in class in a few days. He was looking forward to the grand welcome by his students. He knew he had to do something about Howard, but he should wait until Howard finished the article or maybe a few more articles ... but who was to say Howard wouldn't try to kill him again?

Steve began to concoct a plan.

* * *

After another week of recovery, Steve found himself back at the university. He missed the drive back to the campus and walked down the familiar hall into his office. There were two students in the hall. They had looks of shock on their face.

"What? Aren't you happy to see me after my attempted murder?" asked Steve rhetorically.

"Yes, we are relieved to see that you're fine," the student said with a frown.

"Oh, that's wonderful. I'm not sure how the law school, or you for that matter, would survive without me." Steve threw his head back in laughter as he opened his office door. There were no "get well soon" letters in his mailbox or under his door. Such things did not cross Steve's mind.

He sat at his desk, booted up the computer, and promptly sent an email to Howard: Meet me in my office at 2 p.m. sharp.

Steve leaned back on his office chair and threw his feet on the desk. It was good to be back. After preparing his notes for the day's lectures, Steve began making his way to classes. People stopped in their tracks and watched him. This filled Steve with glee. He was a hero to these people. Look how they admired his strength and resolve. He entered the class and took his place in front of the podium. All eyes were on him. It was time to deliver his message.

"Law students, I have returned from an involuntary sabbatical."

As he said this, Howard walked into the class. With slumped shoulders like a beaten dog, he made his way to his assigned seat bashfully.

"According to doctors, the perpetrator missed vital organs, only piercing my stomach slightly. I was certainly lucky, but it was not simply luck. According to police investigators, some fool hired a fly-by-night gang member to kill me. Well, I'm still here. The police are on the case, interviewing informants and trying to get to the bottom of this. They tell me they are getting close, that it might be a disgruntled student.

"Now, I know I can be hard on you, but I am hard because I want you do the best job possible when you graduate." Steve walked around the classroom. "Many of you have been complaining to the Dean and the other higher-ups that I'm exploiting you. This could not be further from the truth. I'm helping you; you're not helping me. I'm guiding you to become award-winning attorneys. You're ungrateful and if I had my way, I would get rid of each and every one of you. I would replace you with more grateful people. Do you know how fortunate you are to attend this school and to be taught by me? You should be kissing my ass right now, not spreading rumors about me to the Dean. Now, someone has tried to kill me. I blame all of you. Things are going to be different around here. I want the appreciation I deserve."

The classroom was dead silent.

Steve's eyes turned to Howard. "And if I did anything to offend you, or upset you, you can talk to me. I know I'm not the nicest person, but I have your best interests in mind. From now on, I want to hear you say it. So, say it."

"Thank you," said the class collectively.

"Louder," demanded Steve.

"Thank you," screamed the class.

"Louder," demanded Steve, pounding the podium, the microphone blaring loudly.

"Thank you," screamed the class yet again.

"That's more like it," replied a delighted Steve. "Now, let's get started with today's material."

47

HOWARD'S STOMACH HAD BEEN IN KNOTS FOR WEEKS. HIS WIFE almost left him. He blamed it on the alcohol. Isabella forgave him on one condition: he had to go to marriage counseling. But Professor Jones was still alive, as the Calle Ocho gang failed to kill him. Howard still wondered if things would lead back to him. He also worried that Steve would show Isabella the pictures. Howard did not contact the gang again, even though he owed them another ten thousand dollars for the failed hit. He hoped that this would be over.

Howard received an email from Steve: Meet me in my office at 2 p.m. sharp. This was it. He was going to have to meet the very person he tried to kill. But he had to save his marriage. Steve had threatened him with those sordid pictures, and that left him no choice.

Howard made his way to class a little later than usual. He entered and got into his seat while Steve was speaking. Howard's heart was beating loudly in his chest, but he could not focus on the words coming out of Steve's mouth.

Howard saw that Steve was looking at him, so he nodded silently. He was never so grateful for a lecture to begin.

And then the lecture ended. It was 1:45 p.m. and Howard had to make his way to Steve's office. He'd play it cool. How could Steve know it was him? Howard had had nothing to eat all day, and his stomach grumbled loudly.

Howard began to make his way to Steve's office, wishing he'd never cheated on Isabella. Why did he do it?

He arrived at Steve's office at 1:55 p.m. The seconds ticked by like minutes, and the minutes seemed like hours. It was 2 p.m. and Steve would show up any minute now.

2:05 p.m. and still no professor. At 2:22, Steve finally arrived.

"Were you waiting long?" Steve asked with a grin.

"No, just a few minutes," replied Howard.

Steve opened the office and entered. Steve knew full well about their 2 p.m. meeting time, and he knew that Howard would be nervous. He arrived late on purpose, choosing to goof around the halls for almost a half hour, checking stocks, and eating a sandwich.

"What can I do for you?" asked Steve, pretending he had not asked Howard for the meeting.

"You emailed me today, Professor Jones. You wanted to meet at two."

"Ah, yes. I do apologize. It must've slipped my mind. Being almost killed really does something to your psyche. You know, the police say it was a murder-for-hire job. Someone tried to hire someone to kill me. Who would do such a thing? It must be someone who wants to hide something," said Steve casually.

He watched Howard's eyes sink into his skull, taking great pleasure in the beads of sweat appearing on Howard's face. He remained silent for what seemed like a few seconds to him but a millennium to Howard.

Howard was suffering with the silence. He wanted to break it but could only mouth some words. His voice cracked. "Yes, well, it was a shock to many in the student body." He recalled the party he had in celebration.

"Yes, indeed. I'm sure of it. Things like this always seem to affect the young. One of my own professors died of mysterious circumstances. It certainly was no murder though. He was much loved by all, including me. He was so young and fresh. Very much like me. It was hard to see why anyone wanted him murdered ... I mean dead. Ha-ha. There I go confusing my situation with his."

Howard fidgeted in his chair. He wanted this meeting over. "Professor, could we possibly talk about what you wanted me to do today? I'd love to get started on things."

"Of course. First though, I wanted to ask you whether I offended you in any way with those pictures. Being stabbed makes you think of things like blackmail. You know that I still have those photos. I have them locked in a safety deposit box at my bank, along with other things that need securing."

"No-no-no. You were just doing what you thought best. I haven't even thought about that in months. I broke off the relationship with the student. It was just something I did for the thrill of it. You did me a favor. You made me a better person, a better husband, and a better lawyer. The last thing I want to be is corrupt, and I was using my position to satisfy my lust." Howard was on the verge of tears now. He knew that he screwed up big time. His life was over.

Steve got up out of his chair, walked over to the door, and closed it. He turned and stood over Howard.

Howard began to shake uncontrollably.

"Why Howard, you seem to be quite shaken up, you're sweating! What's the matter?"

Howard broke down. He knew that he was done.

"Howard, did you try to kill me?" Steve asked sarcastically.

"No-no, of course not. I'm just under a lot of pressure, that's all," he sobbed.

"Howard. Howard. Howard. Sometimes, we make bad decisions. I had a feeling it was you. You seem intelligent, I'm quite certain of it. Just calm down."

Howard had had enough. He got out of the chair, but Steve pushed him back down. For a professor, Steve was quite strong. He was not built or anything, but his stature gave him leverage over the much shorter and thinner student.

"You aren't going anywhere," laughed Steve at Howard's attempt at retreating. "You're going to tell me exactly what happened. Did you speak with some guy named Pepi?"

"What? No!" Howard yelled.

"Just asking." Steve reassured Howard. "Just making idle conversation. You know he's dead, right? He killed himself. It was on the radio. He put a bullet in his head. I guess the pressure got to him. Gangsters can be such pansies with their teardrop tattoos."

"Can I go? Please. I just want to go," pleaded Howard.

"No, no. Sit a bit, sit a bit." Steve walked back to his desk.

Howard sprang up and turned for the door. Steve had locked it, but it was simple enough to turn the latch and leave. He pulled on the door, furiously turning the handle while sobbing.

Steve looked on and began to laugh maniacally. "Just turn the latch, you fool," he howled.

Howard opened the door and ran out of the office and out of the building. Steve's laughter seemed to chase him. Howard kept running, trying to escape his thoughts and the disaster that was awaiting him. He had no idea what to do, and Steve's haunting laughter continued to wrack his brain.

Back in the office, Steve chuckled to himself and did so for hours on end.

48

DONOVAN WAS PISSED THAT HE HAD TO FOLLOW STEVE AROUND all day while his more senior partners were off on a fun day of fishing. Steve was back in classes and following his basic routine. He was in the middle of office hours. It was incredibly boring work just sitting in the car and watching with a pair of binoculars, eating pork rinds, and drinking soda. He texted Donna every now and then just to break the monotony of it all. She was busy with family but found time to reply. Her uncle and his family were in town, so there was a party going on.

* * *

Carlos and Wayne were out on a boat in the Everglades. So far, they'd caught a medium-sized catfish. They were drinking beer after beer. Wayne was enjoying himself but couldn't forget that Steve had a recording of him breaking into his apartment. He thought maybe he could take people out fishing after he lost his badge. Always good to have a backup plan.

Carlos needed more days like this. He thought of Natasha

and his sister every now and then. Carlos felt a little guilty, but there was nothing he could do except put a tail on Steve.

Wayne felt a tug on his rod and reeled in as fast as he could. Unfortunately, there was nothing on the end of the rod; the fish had somehow taken the bait. "Steve is proving himself to be quite a slippery fish himself," said Wayne as he placed more bait on the hook.

"Yeah, well," was the only thing Carlos said. There was a pause. "All we can do now is wait. Steve is going to slip up somehow, and we'll get him."

"Donovan is a professional. If we keep up the pressure, Steve will get himself caught." The two men took comfort in this, and both eased back in their chairs. There was a calm wind blowing in off the lake. Wayne pointed at two alligators on the bank. He had his gun ready, but there was no need to worry; they were just basking in the warm sun. Carlos looked down at his phone. There were no texts from Donovan. That was good news for now.

Wayne eventually broke the silence and asked, "Why do you think Steve hasn't said anything about the tape of us in his apartment?"

"He's probably going to use it to blackmail us in the future. Or he's going to try to get evidence thrown out of court. I can't see any other reason for him not to report us," responded Carlos.

"That would mean that he knows that we know he's a killer. The way he was talking back in the hospital makes me feel that he's also aware that we know he has us on tape. Should we try to get our hands on the tape?" Wayne wondered if there was any way they could save their jobs.

"No. No more of that. It will only get us deeper into problems. Looks like we have a sort of balancing act. Whatever happens, we need to collect enough evidence to put him away. Or we can do it another way."

Wayne nodded. "Vigilante justice."

"That's the last resort," Carlos stated. "If we can't put a stop to him in court, we can surely do it some other way."

Wayne jumped to his feet. "Now, *that's* what I'm talking about!"

The boat shook violently, and Wayne lost his balance and fell into the water. Carlos keeled over, laughing hysterically. In the chaos, Carlos' phone let out a loud buzzing sound. It was Donovan. Carlos turned stone-faced as he picked up.

"Give me some news I can use."

"Looks like Steve is leaving the office, probably going home as per usual. This guy's life is so uneventful," said Donovan with a sigh.

"Do your job. follow him and let us know what happens."

49

STEVE WAS BACK IN ACTION. HE KEPT HIMSELF BUSY TORTURING students and faculty and taking delight in uncomfortable situations. The semester was almost over and he thought that maybe he could go on a little vacation. He lived in Florida, but he longed for a taste of the island life. When he was in law school, he remembered going to Puerto Rico for a conference. He loved walking on the beach, hiking in the tropical rainforest, and bathing in picturesque waterfalls. The women there were also beautiful, curvaceous, and fun to be around. Yes, it was time for him to take a little vacation.

Steve daydreamed with his feet on the desk. He was supposed to be working on a paper. Instead, he got onto the web and purchased a ticket to Turks and Caicos, a British Overseas Territory. He wanted to see something new and exciting. He printed out the ticket, and the fire alarm began to blare. Steve got out of his chair and left for the front door. He did not smell any smoke, so he knew it would be a false alarm. He calmly walked down the hall and outside. Without thinking, he left his office door open.

Donovan saw people were running outside. He also saw

Steve walk calmly out. Donovan realized that this was his chance. He got out of his car and walked to the back of the building. There was a group forming outside the back of the building, but he walked past them and into the building. Not knowing how much time he had, he jogged quickly up the stairs, passing some frantic-looking professors and students. He made it to Steve's office and closed the door.

As long as the alarm was on, he had a chance to look around. The first place he looked was in the trash. It was empty. He looked on the desk: nothing. The shelves were packed with law books, so he did not bother to search them. Two minutes went by and nothing substantial turned up, and he decided to leave. Just as he made for the door, he saw the printer had a piece of paper sticking out: an airplane ticket to Turks and Caicos. Nice. Maybe he could tail Steve down in paradise. Steve noted the date and time of arrival and departure, then went back to the car.

In the car, Donovan placed another call to Carlos and informed him about the trip. "Your boy is going down to Turks and Caicos as soon as the semester's over."

"You're going down there to keep an eye on him," ordered Carlos

"Yes, sir! I've been dying for an opportunity like this," exclaimed Donovan.

50

THE FIRE ALARM CONTINUED TO SOUND, CREATING A RINGING IN Steve's ears. He was irritated, standing outside in the heat. Firefighters were running into the building with axes, looking around the building and talking to other faculty members.

One was making his way into the building when Steve stood in front of his path. "How long is this going to take? I have very important—"

"Move aside," the firefighter said.

This infuriated Steve; he stood shocked. Some students overheard. Their mouths hung open with a look of glee. This did not escape Steve, adding further embarrassment and anger.

"Typical working-class rudeness," huffed Steve loudly. "I hope you die in a fire."

The firefighter was long gone by then.

Steve stomped off, fuming as he went. People often wondered why he reacted to things in such a negative way. It all boiled down to his childhood experiences and his need to show aggression to protect himself and his ego, one that was now inflated beyond repair. He boiled as he walked and felt the need to take out his anger on something or someone. Yet there was no one around except a few squirrels. After a few minutes, Steve remembered the project with Howard. He needed a progress report. Continuing to use Howard was probably the best course of action, but there were many students clamoring for the opportunity. Torturing Howard would be the best way to get relief from the previous slight.

Walking to the cafeteria and back, Steve thought of different ways to get back at Howard for arranging his stabbing. By the time he arrived back at the office, he had already thought of one. Entering his office, he was surprised that his door was open. He could not remember whether he closed it or not, but nothing seemed missing or moved. His computer logged out after five minutes, so no harm no foul. However, Steve did note a smell. A smell of pork rinds. Maybe one of those disgusting firefighters had come in there.

Steve sat down, threw his feet on his desk and dialed Howard. After a few rings, he picked up.

"Hello, S-s-teve," Howard stammered.

"What? That's professor to you, or Dr. Jones. What's wrong with you, Howard?"

"Oh, yes, my fault, sir. What can I do for you?"

"Yes, well, not much, I think, except some stress. How's progress going on the article? I want to see your progress in the next five minutes."

"I haven't been able to work on it. I've had some personal issues I needed to work out."

"What's wrong, Howard? Oh, did she find out that you've been, oh, how do the rappers put it? A trifling ho'? That you've been creeping about?"

"No, just been unwell."

"Ah yes, I understand now. Our last meeting disturbed me greatly. Since you haven't made any progress, I'd like to hand the rest of the assignment to someone else, just to get it completed. This says nothing about you, I just think you need some time to focus on your own mess of a life."

"Yes, sir, thank you. That takes some pressure off."

"You will remain an author, but not second. You'll be the third author."

"But we just have one more section to finish. I did five by myself, and that's the majority of the work," Howard protested.

"Howie, Howie, Howie," Steve stated in a patronizing voice. "You know nothing about the publishing business. How can I ever recruit someone new at this stage without promising them something worth their time? I mean, come on. Stop thinking about yourself for once in your life and see the bigger picture here. I don't have to tell you that, given how you've treated your own wife. I guess I can't expect much from someone like you, as you have no self-control."

There was silence on the phone. Howard knew that all this was true. He had done this to himself. He had now lost the project he was depending on. He finally replied, "Yes, you're right."

"That's good. Now, stop blabbering. Email me what you have, and I'll pass it on to the next person."

"Yes sir, I'll do that right now," said Howard.

"Very good." Steve hung up.

Howard was stunned but not overly shocked or disappointed. The past few weeks had been an absolute whirlwind. He knew nothing was going to get better any time soon. His despair was manageable. Howard and Isabella were working out their problems, and things were getting better. Being hopeful helped Howard. He had to change, and all this was punishment, which he fully accepted. Howard placed down his phone, went to his computer and sent Steve the work he had been toiling away on for months.

Steve felt satisfied. He had a plan for Howard, a slow and painful one. Steve did not have to kill to gain pleasure. Causing mental anguish and despair was also fun for him. Steve was left with the task of finding Howard's replacement. He poked his head out of his office and saw a student, a young lady that seemed to be in a trance. Steve did not recognize her at all.

"Hey, you," Steve called to the woman.

"Yes, Dr. Jones?"

"Oh, so you know me. Are you a law student at this university?"

"Why yes. I'm in the afternoon session. I sit in the back ..."

Steve interrupted. "Great. Well, come in a moment, I have a once-in-a-lifetime opportunity for you." Steve had a big smirk on his face.

51

CARLOS AND WAYNE WERE HAPPY THAT THINGS WERE FINALLY moving along. As they packed up their cars after a day of fishing, the two sang a disco song. They were happy, happier than they had been in a long time.

* * *

Donovan was looking forward to his trip to his tropical paradise. It was still a few weeks away, and it would still be work, but he wanted to get away badly. He told Donna his story, but instead of being happy, she was worried. As soon as Donovan had the chance, he called and tried to clarify the mission. Donna was not convinced. Her love was following a potential serial killer to an island. It did not make much sense to her. Why not wait until he returned? Were Donovan and the police officers overstepping their bounds or breaking any laws?

Donna had some major concerns that Donovan brushed off as non-important. This led to a huge argument over their future ... that Donovan was "not listening again." The conversation ended on a tense note, and Donovan was angry. He went for a long walk to calm down. He thought about his future with Donna, and what she'd said about the trip—whether it was even necessary.

He called Carlos, who reassured him that it was indeed important. It would be helpful to see what Steve was doing down in Turks and Caicos. Both Carlos and Wayne said they would do it themselves if it were not for "other commitments", a very vague statement. Deep down, Donovan wanted to go. It was good for his career to get some field experience.

Two weeks passed quickly, and the day of the trip finally arrived. Both Steve and Donovan packed their bags and departed for the airport around the same time. Donovan grew a beard and wore large sunglasses to disguise his face. They would be on the same direct flight. The plane itself was a regional vessel with enough room for about one hundred people.

Steve was looking forward to the trip after a very eventful semester. He felt like he deserved a vacation more than anyone. He did not feel much pain from the stabbing, and that was quite a relief. Steve used the incident to his advantage, calling in sick every now and then, and having visiting professors teach the classes for him. He promised them coauthored pieces of which they would do most, if not all, the work. As he slid into the taxi to the airport, he felt a great sense of satisfaction.

Donovan patched things up with Donna and promised that when he got back, he would put in a request for vacation time and come see her. Donna sobbed for joy, and this made Donovan feel that all was not lost. He knew he was not the perfect guy and was glad he'd met Donna.

Carlos dropped him at the airport and gave him a quick rundown of what to look for, what to do, and what to expect. They knew that what they were doing was not completely legal, but it was worth the effort to collect evidence, even if it was inadmissible in court.

At the airport, both Steve and Donovan cleared security without any problems. Steve went to have breakfast at a café, and Donovan drank coffee in a coffee shop opposite. Donovan watched Steve, pretending to read a magazine as Steve drank mimosa after mimosa. He wondered whether Steve would make it on the plane; the guy had the tolerance of a bull moose.

Steve was not a big drinker but thought it would be fun to try a mimosa. He saw other people drinking it and thought that maybe it would be good. For breakfast, he ordered the largest thing on the menu called the Big-Boy Breakfast: three eggs, four slabs of bacon, hashbrowns, toast, and fried tomatoes. He knew this would give him bad gas, especially with the alcohol.

For Steve, part of the fun of traveling was breaking wind on a plane. This was amusing for two reasons. First, no one would know who was doing it, as people would be closely packed together. Even in first class, no one would know who the culprit was. Second, and for Steve this was the kicker, even if people could narrow down the guilty party, there was no way to get off the plane. Everyone had to sit there and suffer for the entire flight. Steve chuckled to himself, as he would soon be ruining people's enjoyment.

After breakfast, Steve walked over to the gate to board the flight. Donovan followed, making sure to stay ample distance away. Steve wore an obnoxious straw hat which made Donovan's job all the easier. Steve took his seat and dozed off. Donovan decided to do the same.

After what seemed like an eternity at the gate, it was finally time to board the plane. Steve was happy that he'd booked a first-class ticket, while Donovan rode in coach. Steve boarded first, and Donovan watched as Steve stumbled through the line and onto the gateway. He was clearly inebriated, but he took his seat. The stewardess offered him another drink, and Steve gladly obliged. He was in a good mood and as long as the flight attendants knew their place, he had no issues.

Donovan followed about twenty minutes later. By the time Donovan made it inside the plane, Steve was fast asleep. An empty glass sat on his tray table. Donovan laughed to himself. Easiest job he'd ever had.

Through the flight, Donovan watched a movie but kept an eye open. Steve was in his seat, fast asleep—or so people thought. Every now and then, he would lift his leg and squeeze out a fart like he was in his living room. The travelers next to him were not happy. They paid extra to receive first-class service, and the experience was ruined. To add insult to injury, Steve would laugh to himself as one might sleep-laugh. However, Steve was just pretending. He knew he was a sociopath, and he accepted it.

The two-hour flight finally came to an end, and both men cleared customs without issue. Steve called for a cab to get to his hotel. Donovan instructed his cab to follow Steve's. The resort Steve was staying in was a four-star hotel on the beach and cost five hundred dollars a night. Once Donovan noted Steve's hotel, he bribed the concierge for information about Steve, his booked activities, and any movement. He then took the cab to his cheap motel room somewhere downtown.

Checking in was an absolute nightmare. There was no one at the front desk for twenty minutes. A short, overweight woman soon arrived, looked at Donovan without acknowledging him, and sat down. She was sweating profusely in the tropical heat and was miserable. Donovan broke the silence and asked to be checked in. After typing away at the computer and without asking for Donovan's name, she silently handed him some keys.

Donovan did not bother asking for directions to his room. After some exploring, he found it and entered. A blast of hot air emerged from the room. For some reason, the air conditioning was set on heat. He fought his way to the thermostat and set it to the lowest possible setting. The room smelled of old cigarettes and marijuana.

Donovan sat on the bed and laughed to himself. Great, no pool and now this. It couldn't get any worse. Donovan pulled out his laptop and wrote two messages. The first was to Donna to let her know he arrived safely and that the room was lovely. The second was to Carlos. It read:

Carlos,

   The Eagle has landed and is safe in his luxury hotel. I'm in the fifth circle of hell in this motel. I "spoke" to the bellhop and he will inform me of Steve's movements. The room is shit. You guys owe me big time for this.

Donovan then made his way to Steve's hotel to keep an eye on him.

On the other side of the island, Steve's room had a balcony overlooking the pool and the beach. The woman at the front desk welcomed him with a refreshing punch made with some locally made rum, orange juice, a splash of grenadine, and a twist of lime. The resort had everything one would need for a fun vacation including three pools, five bars, three restaurants, and a massage parlor.

As he made his way to his room, Steve noted beautiful women everywhere, sunbathing and sipping cocktails. Steve spotted one gorgeous brunette reading a book and wasted no time. After arriving at the room and not tipping the bellhop, he threw his bags aside, put on a pair of trunks, and headed to the pool.

Steve was tall and in good shape, or so he saw himself. He was thin with a bit of a potbelly. He sucked in his gut and walked past the brunette. She did not glance up, which frustrated Steve. How could anyone not notice this Adonis? He walked over to the bar and ordered another rum punch. Steve then waltzed over to a deck chair and sprawled out.

Donovan walked into the pool area. He told the hotel staff that he was there to have lunch with a friend. He found Steve and sat at the restaurant just across from the pool. He saw Steve take a long sip of his rum punch and felt a bit jealous. Here he was, having a miserable time following that psycho, and Steve was living it up.

Steve watched the brunette, and soon she got up and walked past him.

"Hello, gorgeous! Want to really have a good time?" greeted Steve.

The woman tsked loudly, ignoring Steve's greeting and continued to her deck chair to tan in the sun.

Wow, what an absolute bitch! How dare she ignore him! *No one* ignored him. Steve looked down at his stomach and saw the stab wound. She must have thought he was some sort of hoodlum with that scar. That Howard. He swore he would torture that boy even more now. He might even kill that precious wife of his, and then him. Howard had messed with the wrong guy. Steve swallowed the rest of his drink, then walked over to the brunette.

"Hey! Check this out," exclaimed Steve as he cannonballed into the pool. The water doused the woman and everyone else who happened to be around. Steve's head broke the surface. His toothy grin was from ear to ear.

The woman was appalled, her hair was completely ruined. Children were clapping in delight. Donovan could not believe his eyes. A grown man, a man educated by the finest institutions in the world, had lowered himself to that of a spoiled child. Donovan watched as management intervened quickly with towels for the poor woman. The head manager was also summoned. In a matter of moments, the head manager approached Steve, looking annoyed.

"Excuse me, sir. Please do not engage in any horseplay in or around the pool. It is my responsibility to ensure the safety and enjoyment of all guests," advised the manager.

"My deepest apologies. It'll never happen again. I promise," said Steve mockingly, using the most sarcastic voice he could muster.

"I reserve the right to remove you from the hotel. Please refrain from any further disorder."

Steve turned away and became quiet. He was boiling inside. Steve did not want to be thrown out of the hotel, but he did not like the tone of the manager's voice. He'd have to write a very harsh review after the vacation was over. The next person to cross him would be dead.

Donovan, on the other hand, bore witness to all this. He stared in disbelief and did not notice the waiter asking him if he was ready to order. Donovan ordered a forty-dollar burger and fries and made sure to get the receipt. Carlos was going to pay through the nose. If this entertainment kept up, the trip might not be so bad after all.

52

THE NEXT DAY, STEVE BOOKED A TOUR TO SEE THE ISLAND. THE bellhop Donovan bribed called to inform him of the move. The tour was a public affair, so there was no need for tracking. Donovan noted this in the journal. Steve was due back in the evening, so Donovan booked a table at Steve's hotel's restaurant. Donovan assumed that Steve would have dinner at the hotel.

He spent the day walking about town and seeing the island. He also phoned Donna to catch up. The two had a pleasant conversation. It ended with both saying, "I love you". After, Donovan went over to Steve's hotel to have dinner and do surveillance.

Steve's tour of the island was uneventful. He wished he'd never booked the tour. His mood had remained negative since yesterday's rejection and confrontation. He ate no breakfast and avoided eye contact with anyone. The tour guide showed them around the town, and people took in the history of the island. While everyone was enjoying the tour, Steve was bored.

The tour ended with a visit to a gift shop. It was a small

place in desperate need of repair. There was an old woman at the counter who owned the place. She was famous on the island for her longevity as a store owner, working with her father as a child and continuing even today. Tourists were busy looking around at the items. Steve browsed, eyeing all the objects.

One thing caught his eye: a replica Taino knife made of animal bone. The Taino people were the indigenous people of the island. Since the knife was made of bone, it would not set off any alarms at the airport. Steve asked the old lady to see the knife, which she produced with a smile.

The knife was finely crafted from a single bone. It was broad from the handle and narrowed down to a sharp point. It was colored white with an illustration of the sun at the very tip. Steve wanted that knife. The old lady watched Steve admire her knife until another tourist asked a question about a conch shell.

Looking around, Steve quickly placed the knife in his underwear, neatly between his butt cheeks. He continued to walk around the shop. The old lady returned, and Steve distracted her with a question about a cheap Rastafarian wig. Steve put on the charm and danced around for the old lady with the wig saying things like "yeah mon, 'ere me now. I Rastafari."

This distracted the old lady long enough that he bought the wig and walked out, disappearing into the crowd. He took the knife out in glee and wondered whether it would get any action. If he killed someone on this trip, this bad boy would be his favorite souvenir. He placed the knife in his pocket and made his way toward his tour bus.

Steve was glad to return to the hotel in the evening, as he was starving. He went downstairs to the restaurant and waited to be seated. Donovan was already there. Steve sat down at a table and looked around. He was feeling lonely and frustrated. There were happy couples all around, young and beautiful. They were smiling and laughing over cocktails, appetizers, and entrees. What were these people so happy about? *Look at those fools.*

It would be so easy to force his way into the kitchen, grab a butcher knife, and slice those smiles from their stupid faces. That would certainly make them remember how much fun they had. Steve grunted out loud. He noticed a man, Donovan, sitting alone like he was. He wondered why he was alone. The waiter arrived and took his order: a Scotch and a beer, lobster bisque to start, and filet mignon as the main course.

Donovan overheard Steve's order and became instantly jealous. He ordered a glass of water and another burger with fries. Donovan watched Steve swallow his Scotch and beer and order another and another. Clearly, the man was determined to get wasted and was paying a premium to do so.

In twenty minutes, Steve had consumed five glasses of whiskey and two beers. The waiters brought over the bisque he ordered, but he was so drunk at that point, he did not want it. He was so focused on his loneliness that he forgot where he was. He thought about his bitch ex-wife and how he did not care enough to work on his marriage. He was fixated on the happy couples. And he also felt some degree of empathy for Donovan, not because he felt sorry for Donovan, but because they were both alone. Realizing this, Steve decided to go over and introduce himself. He told the waiter that he was switching tables.

He got up and walked over to Donovan's table. Donovan was in the middle of thanking the waiter for bringing his dinner when he looked up. There was Steve standing over him.

"Hey, there. Mind if I join you?"

"Uh-uh, no, not at all, please." Donovan was shocked. Did he recognize him from the plane? What did he want with him?

Steve sat down with a thud. "Man, I hate all these couples. It makes me sick. I can't enjoy myself. I mean, here we are in the middle of paradise, alone, and there are all these happy people. It's like they want to piss me off."

"Yeah well, it's just one of those things. My name is Jacob," replied Donovan.

"Jacob? You down with the tribe?" asked Steve.

"What?" Donovan was confused by the question.

"Are you Jewish? Not that it's a bad thing," Steve replied. He was always awkward with conversations.

"No, I'm not Jewish. I'm not anything," replied Donovan, who was feeling more comfortable now. Steve was just drunk and lonely. He'd play it cool.

"So, what are you here for?" asked Steve, trying to change the subject.

"Vacation. I had some free time at work."

"Oh yeah? What do you do?"

"I'm a sales representative at a—"

Steve quickly cut him off. "I'm a professor at Southeastern University Law School in South Miami. Bet you've never spoken to a law professor before in your line of work," boasted Steve.

"No. I certainly haven't had the pleasure," replied Donovan curtly.

"Yeah well, I'm a big deal down there. I'm known nationwide."

"Oh yeah?"

"I'm world famous. I'm here on vacation, but like you I'm flying solo," said Steve, putting his hands behind his head and leaning back in his chair.

Donovan was still in shock at what had transpired. He was supposed to watch Steve, not fraternize. Steve was waiting on Donovan to respond, so Donovan said the first thing that popped into his mind. "What did you order?"

"You know what I hate?" asked Steve, completely ignoring Donovan's question. "I hate having to see these couples. I mean, yeah, you're happy, but just wait. That bliss lasts a few months, reality sets in and boom: divorce. I've seen it a thousand times."

Donovan realized he had nothing to worry about. Steve was drunk and probably would not remember him or the "conversation" they were having. He finally felt relaxed enough to take a bite of his burger. There was an interesting spice to it that he enjoyed. What an interesting situation. He wondered what Carlos and Wayne would say if they could see him now; Wayne would keep his responses short, as he had no idea what would set Steve off.

"I see you got the burger. I got filet mignon with the lobster bisque to start. Hope it comes sometime this century."

"Living the dream, huh, Steve?" Donovan took another bite.

"Oh yeah, oh yeah. It's good to be me, I work really hard and..." Steve stopped talking, freezing completely. His eyes were as large as the dinner plates on the table.

Donovan stopped chewing. "Are you ok? What's wrong?"

"Nothing. Nothing. Nothing. Everything's great. I just remembered something. Just give me a second," replied Steve, clearly shaken. Steve thought hard. He had not introduced himself. He never introduced himself. He made that a point; no one needed to know his name. How did this guy know his name? What the hell was going on? And who was this guy?

Donovan was puzzled, but he took Steve's word for it.

Steve sat stone-faced and gazed at him for what seemed like an eternity. Donovan took another bite of burger.

The waiter finally came and placed Steve's bisque in front of him. Steve suddenly got up and walked over to the bathroom at a snail's pace. Steve made it to the bathroom and stared into the mirror. His thoughts were jumbled. Could those officers be following him all the way down here? How did they know he was going to be there? There was a noose around his neck. He needed to find out what was going on. He had to compose himself, go back out there, and try to figure out that guy Jacob.

Steve washed his face and sat down in a stall. He remembered the Taino knife in his pocket. He took it out and stared at it. He knew what he had to do. He then got up and walked over to the table.

53

STEVE RETURNED TO THE TABLE AND SAT DOWN. HE STOPPED drinking for the evening. He asked the waiter to reheat his bisque and keep his filet mignon warm. It was a beautiful cut, and Steve did not want to waste both dishes. He ate with Donovan and spoke about movies, sports, and so on. Donovan had finished and wanted to excuse himself several times, but Steve would not let him go until he finished his meal. After the meal, Steve finally allowed Donovan to leave the table and restaurant.

Steve followed Donovan to the hotel's taxi stand and departed. Donovan gave his hotel's address to the manager, got into a taxi, and drove off. Steve then returned to the taxi stand and got Donovan's address from the manager. He went back to his hotel room and collapsed on the floor, shaken to his core. He had managed to play it cool during the evening, but alone in the hotel room, he sobbed. His fear soon turned into anger. Taking his new knife out of his pocket, he concocted a plan and calmed down after a few moments.

Steve had to find out who this Jacob really was.

* * *

Back in the hotel room, Donovan wrote an email to Carlos about the events of the evening. He then wrote Donna a quick message, watched the local news, and went to bed. He had trouble sleeping after the events of the evening. He could not help but feel something had gone wrong, especially given Steve's sudden silence at dinner. Donovan could sense Steve's uneasiness but tried to remember that Steve's attitude changed after returning from the bathroom. Maybe he had an upset stomach after all that drinking? He'd probably puked in the bathroom and felt better. Donovan closed his eyes and fell asleep.

Donovan was choked awake. There was something pressing on his neck. He was gagged and he could not move. He was tied together tightly with bedsheets; each leg was tied to a bed post. A head popped up from under the bed. It was Steve, putting the final knots on the sheet together.

"Oh? Too tight? Hello, Jacob, or is it Donovan?"

Donovan let out a muffled scream.

Steve jeeringly placed a cupped hand to his ear. "I'm sorry, what's that?"

Donovan continued to let out muffled screams, but it was all in vain.

Steve continued, his voice and expression calm. "You don't know how easy it is to get information in this country. People simply don't care about security. They are so unmotivated to do a good job, so there is no one at the front desk. The logbook was right there for anyone to see, how lucky. I saw no Jacob and was about to leave the hotel."

Steve's face grew red with rage. "I figured you were here to follow me. There are three people booked in this shithole of a hotel with my checkout date. One was a woman, clearly not you. Another name was Chinese. So that leaves you. But what

199

made me super lucky was the fact that the front desk has the master key for all the rooms. I can get into any room I want. I'm glad I'm here with you yet again tonight."

Steve stood up and walked around the room, taking great pleasure in Donovan's scared state.

Donovan was shaking violently. He thought of Donna and wished he had never come to the island. He began to pray, which was something he had not done in years. He knew what was going to happen.

"What? Don't you feel the same way?" asked Steve. He suddenly pushed his face up to Donovan's and whispered, "I never, ever, ever gave you my name. I told you where I worked but I never gave you my name. How did you know it? Don't answer. I'm going to have a quick look around your room."

Steve rummaged through the closet and soon found something that looked like a leather wallet under some socks in the top drawer. Steve opened the wallet and found a badge with the engraving "Miami PD".

"A little outside your jurisdiction, huh? What's your name again? Donavan? What are you doing, following me around? I'm just on a lovely vacation. This must be that Latino cop and cowboy team that's been sniffing around my apartment. You know this is harassment? I could have you all fired, but I'm waiting for the right moment. But you know, right now, I have a little problem. Maybe you can help me out?"

Donovan's eyes darted around the room. He began to pull on his restraints, but they were tight. His wrists were turning red.

Steve continued, "The problem is that if you turn up dead, I might get in more trouble, and I don't want that. I just can't let you go, though. You'll just run ahead and say I did all this. I just want to know something. Why are the cops following me? I'm an innocent man, I've done nothing wrong. Just shake your head for no and nod for yes. Do you understand?"

Donovan nodded.

"Are you following me because I'm suspected of some wrongdoing?"

Donovan nodded.

"Was it because of the disappearance of my student Natasha?"

Donovan nodded again.

"Did those two cops I mentioned, I believe their first names were Carlos and Wayne, send you here?"

Donovan nodded a fourth time.

Steve understood that he was now under suspicion. He got up from the bed, walked into the bathroom, and looked into the mirror. His hair dangled down his face. He had bags under his eyes; the dark circles seemed to accentuate his stress under the bright, fluorescent light. If he killed this guy, Wayne and Carlos were going to get even more suspicious. It made no sense for him to make things worse. Those cops had it in for him, and they wouldn't stop until they either put him in prison or killed him. They were already breaking laws to track him, breaking into his apartment, and following him down there.

Steve returned into the bedroom. He looked at Donovan, who had managed get one of his legs free. Steve laughed and walked over. "Gosh, what am I going to do with you? I like your spirit, kid. You remind me a little bit of myself. No matter what happens, you've got to keep fighting till the last minute. I'm not going to hurt you, although I would love to teach you a lesson about keeping within the limits of the law. You aren't cut out for this business. You better get out now while you still can."

Steve sat down at the desk and turned on Donovan's computer. "Let's see what's on your social media, old boy? Let me learn a little about you so I can figure out a nice solution for this little mess you made."

Donovan forced his head up to see what Steve was doing on his computer.

Without a word, Steve brought over the laptop so that he could enter a password. Steve then logged onto Donovan's email and saw the correspondence with Carlos. He logged onto a messenger service and saw the messages to Donna.

"Ah! Love! But she lives all the way in the Philippines. My goodness. She's adorable!" Steve looked through Donovan's files and saw a folder labeled "Donna". "Hey Donovan, are these going to be racy photos? Maybe I shouldn't look at these, hmm?"

Steve opened the file and gazed at the photos and gasped. "Well, well, Donovan, you devil, you. What an absolute babe! What are you doing following me, an innocent *man*, on his vacation when you should be with your love?"

Steve plopped himself on the bed beside Donovan. He placed two hands under his chin and gazed deep into his eyes as if he were a pre-teen girl. "You know, you should be with her in the Philippines. Why be a cop when you can take your meager savings and live like a king over there? If I let you go, would you go? Would you be with your Donna?"

Donovan nodded energetically.

"How can I trust you? You're a dirty cop, after all."

Donovan signaled for Steve to take out his gag.

"If you make a sound, I'm going to punch you right in the throat, understood?"

Donovan nodded.

Steve took out the gag, and Donovan coughed and licked his dry lips. He managed to get out, "I'll go, I'll go. Book my ticket for tomorrow. You'll never see me again. I'll never again enter the United States."

Steve looked at Donovan with a skeptical grin. He then walked over to the laptop and booked a ticket to the Philippines for Donovan. After some time, Steve broke the silence. "Alright, I got you a ticket to Manila for the day after tomorrow. You'll have to find your way to Donna's place after that. I should have asked what the closest airport was but, oops, I'm taking your laptop as insurance ... but I'd like you to admit your wrongdoing and apologize."

Donovan spent the next five minutes confessing that he broke the law spying on Steve, and that Carlos and Wayne had sent him on this mission.

"If anything happens to me, you will bring down Carlos, Wayne, and the privacy of your precious Donna. Everything you love and respect will be tarnished forever. I want you on that plane." Steve placed the gag back into Donovan's mouth and gave him a light slap on the face. "I'm going to leave now. Housekeeping will be around soon to free you. Be on that plane. Oh, I need your credit card login information. As soon as you land, buy something. If you don't, kiss your girl's privacy goodbye. *Capiche*?"

Donovan quickly nodded and typed up the credit card's username and password.

Steve then leaned over and kissed Donovan gently on the forehead and said, "*Bon voyage*, Donny boy. And would you do me a favor? Have a happy life."

Steve then exited the room with the laptop. Donovan let out a huge sigh. He looked over at the clock. It was only 1 a.m. and it would be another fifteen hours until room service would come to free him.

Steve went back to his hotel, satisfied with the day's events. He walked over to the pool and sat on the deck. He wanted to kill Donovan, but he understood that he was already under real suspicion by the cops. He had to curb his nature and keep his eyes on the bigger prize: keeping his freedom and life as a law professor intact. Killing a cop would only bring further heat.

A waiter came over and he ordered a Cuban cigar. Steve loved cigars and Cubans were his favorite. He could only get inferior Dominican cigars back in Miami. The waiter obliged. Steve lit his cigar and tasted victory.

* * *

After an awkward explanation, Donovan was released by housekeeping. Since Steve took his laptop, he used his cell phone to email Carlos. He wrote two words: I quit. He then wrote Donna: Baby, I'll be home tomorrow. I hate my job. I just want to be with you forever.

Right after, he received a call from Carlos. Donovan let it ring until it went to voicemail. Carlos called again and again. Donovan, seeing that the police part of his life was over, took a walk down to the town's main pier. He looked out at the horizon. Donovan thought he would not have seen the sunrise once again, and yet he was here. Carlos called again and Donovan picked up.

"Carlos."

"Donovan! What the hell is going on? Why aren't you picking up the phone? What do you mean you quit?"

"Look. I'm sick of this job, and I'm sick of you and people like you: police officers, my superiors. You always think you know what's best for everyone. Just because you enforce the law doesn't mean you're above it. You made me follow Steve here, and he's done nothing except eat and drink. I'm not happy, and I hate this life. I'm quitting the force and going to live with my girlfriend in the Philippines." Donovan hung up and threw the phone into the ocean.

Carlos was dumbfounded. He tried calling Donovan a few times but gave up. He slammed his phone on the ground and began to curse.

54

WAYNE WATCHED THE GROWING STORM ON THE HORIZON FROM his boat. He was fishing alone, trying to get a few moments of quiet to himself. Carlos was frustrated with the Steve investigation and was difficult to be around. Donovan's sudden resignation had sent him into an emotional tailspin. Wayne wondered why Donovan would give up his future in the United States to go live with some woman in a foreign country.

He chuckled to himself, remembering the stress of the job. Living far away from all this was certainly an attractive option. Wayne reeled in his line and threw out another cast. He had not caught anything the entire afternoon. He'd get a break. Carlos would get a break. Sooner or later, Steve would slip up. Everyone slipped up now and then. They'd get him.

He got a bite. He slowly placed his feet on his chair's stirrups. Licking his lips, he chugged what remained of his beer and threw the can in the boat. He pulled on his line and felt the fish fight. "Gotcha!" shouted Wayne.

He reeled in but the fish gave him serious resistance. Wayne grunted. What a huge bitch! He leaned back, pulling with all his strength, but then the line unexpectedly went slack.

Wayne fell out of his chair and hit his head on the side of the boat. He was conscious but in pain. He lay there for several minutes.

Getting up, he touched the back of his head with his hand. There was no blood. Dazed, he reeled in his rod. The fish had snapped the line, taking the hook and sinker with it. Wayne cracked open another beer and reached for his phone. Noting the time, he began to pack up and head for home.

Carlos was at the hospital, visiting his twin sister Missy. She was in poor physical and mental health. Still in the psych ward, it was clear that she had made no progress. She could talk, but her focus kept returning to her missing daughter, Natasha. Carlos told her that real progress was being made on the case. It was a lie, however, and she knew it. He could not bear to see his sister like this. He tried to reassure her one last time, but it was no use. Carlos left Missy sobbing.

In the evening, Carlos and Wayne got together for dinner to discuss the case, specifically what could have happened in the Turks and Caicos, and some possible next steps. They met at a busy Cuban restaurant. The hostess took them to a quiet table. Carlos pulled out a notepad while Wayne looked over the menu.

"Here's what we have so far ... Donovan goes down to Turks and Caicos. Donovan checks in the first night and the second night with nothing substantial to report. The next day he quits. It is obvious to me that Steve got to him," said Carlos with a deep frown.

A short, thin, and bald man brought a basket of buttered bread to the table.

Wayne took two pieces and shoved them into his mouth. "I agree," he responded, voice muffled. "Steve let him go. Probably knew that we were following him. He's a smart guy. He must have realized that if he killed Donovan, we'd come after him."

"Yes. He knows we've been operating with some freedom.

He has a lot of dirt on us already. I think we need to ease up a bit."

Wayne was taken by surprise. "Really? You think so? I mean, we have him on the run."

"Yeah, I've been thinking, he knows we're on to him, so he's going to be really careful. Here's what I think—"

Carlos was interrupted by the waiter. They both ordered *Vaca Frita* with rice, a typical Cuban dish of fried steak, beans, and rice.

"Imagine living in Coova mang," joked Wayne.

"As a member of the Cuban community, I'm quite offended," laughed Carlos.

"I got octopus coming out of my eyes 'cause of Castro. *Libertad* mang, like Jimmy Carter says." Wayne was glad he'd managed to get Carlos to smile.

"I wish that movie never came out," chuckled Carlos. "Anyway, back to business. We need a strategy."

"Carlos, maybe we can ease up? Cut him some slack? I was fishing earlier today and had this big guy on the line. I really pulled hard, you know, trying to reel him in, and my line broke, the tackle and everything gone. Sometimes, you have to let the fish think he's in charge, give him some freedom and then, when he least expects it, reel him in and fast. He'll be so confused; his head will spin."

Carlos became quiet. He was thinking the same thing. He looked around the restaurant and saw the faces of the people. Some were happy, others were more solemn and somber. He looked at his partner and replied, "We're on the same page."

"What do we do? Do we monitor his phones, internet search history? Do we put another tail on him?"

"Nothing. We do nothing. We wait. Sometimes, that's the whole job: waiting for the right moment. I think we've been forcing things to happen. It's time to back off a bit and see what happens."

"That works for me," said Wayne, watching a waitress with two plates go to another table. He added, "He'll slip up. No matter how smart a person is, they always manage to screw up."

Carlos picked up the last slice of buttered bread from the basket. He ate it in silence, thinking about the mistakes he'd made throughout this whole investigation. They should have never broken into Steve's apartment and sent Donovan to the islands. He closed his eyes and said a prayer for wisdom, opened them and discovered that the food arrived. Carlos took this as a good sign.

Wayne was already digging in. It would be his first real meal in days, and that first bite would be unforgettable.

55

STEVE HAD ANOTHER TWO DAYS IN TURKS AND CAICOS. ON THE final day, he logged into Donovan's credit card transactions using Donovan's laptop. Steve discovered that a purchase had been made at the Manila airport. Steve laughed to himself as he closed the laptop. He felt good and chuckled as he packed the laptop into his bag. "Another souvenir from de islan' mon."

He gazed at the Taino knife he'd stolen and signed. He wanted to use it on Donovan but convinced himself that murdering him was not a good idea in the long term. Another time. It'd be too obvious. They would know. It was nice to ruin someone's career. That would be his consolation prize.

Steve continued to laugh to himself. He managed to best Carlos yet again, and this brought him enormous satisfaction. Yet the fact that the officers even suspected him was a cause for worry. They had followed him down to Turks and Caicos and this shook Steve to his core.

Steve shuddered as he packed up the rest of his belongings. Prison was not an option. As a lawyer by training, he knew the harsh conditions of the prison system. He knew about the gangs, and the rampant levels of racism plaguing the corrections system. He knew that word would get around that he was wealthy. Predators would extort him for money.

Steve thought of himself as an attractive man and wondered if he would become someone's *Suzie*, someone that would be passed around for sexual favors due to perceived weakness. He would have to pay a gang to protect him. Having no friends or family in his life, he would be all alone. Steve stopped packing and threw himself on the bed. He smelled the clean sheets and stared at his phone.

If he wanted, he could order room service and enjoy delightful Caribbean dishes, an American breakfast, pizza at any time, or a cheeseburger. All that would be taken away in prison. There would be no room service, and the food would be so disgusting, with prisoners relying on commissary. He began to imagine the horrors of prison life, the nutraloaf, the communal showers, the possibility of being raped, hurt, or killed, the complete lack of privacy, and the constant commotion. Steve's thoughts quickly worked him into hysteria. He jumped out of bed, grabbed the hotel room key, and rushed for the door. He'd go to the hotel gym to work out the stress.

The gym was an empty room. No one exercised on vacation. Steve took to the treadmill and began walking at a steady pace. He needed to get his mind off the fear of being caught. Yet the thought of all the people he killed just in the past year alone continued to rack his brain. Natasha came to mind. She was beautiful and young, with a delightful smile. Steve felt an emotion he had not experienced in many years: the sadness that came with regret.

He increased the level of intensity and his walk turned into a jog, then a run. Steve began to sweat, and it relieved some pressure. He began to feel a pit in his stomach and that turned into rumbling, and then pain. Steve refused to focus on it, choosing to keep running. After five minutes, he grew increasingly nauseous and turned off the machine.

His sweat felt cold, and his stomach tightened. Another flash of Natasha's face entered his mind, which increased his level of nervousness. Steve salivated and knew he was going to throw up. He rushed to a nearby trash can and bent over. He spat, heaved, and then released a torrent into the trash can. Just then, a young hotel employee entered the room.

"Sir, are you okay? Shall I get a doctor?"

There was no answer from Steve, who was too busy tasting the contents of last night's dinner. After a long moment, Steve looked up at him. "I'm fine, just a bit sick from that Indian curry you folks cooked up. The spices probably covered up the poor meat quality. I'm a lawyer, I can have this entire place shut down and you fired. You're quite rude, you know. Leave me alone."

Steve was embarrassed and felt the need to hurt others.

The worker rolled his eyes, quietly exited the gym, and waited outside to clean up the mess.

Steve wiped his mouth with a clean white gym towel. He got up and slowly walked back to his room. After he took a shower, he went to bed and fell asleep.

56

HOWARD AND ISABELLA WERE NOT THE HAPPY COUPLE THEY USED to be. Isabella held Howard in contempt and refused to speak to him respectfully. She wondered why she'd married him in the first place. Her family had warned her of his flirting, and she should have taken that as a sign.

Howard was sorry for what he did and wanted so much to make things right, but Isabella was hardly speaking to him. They were not sleeping in the same room. Howard was at a loss, but he knew he deserved it. He was lucky that she even wanted him in the same house. The baby would be born soon. The pressure was unbearable.

Isabella wanted to give Howard another chance, but realized she also had to become more independent, just in case Howard refused to change. She was a salesperson in the shoe department at a luxury department store. The pay was good, and so were the benefits. Isabella enjoyed her work and loved following all the styles that came with it. She had met Howard at the shoe store; she was helping him with a purchase when she caught him staring at her figure. They were instantly attracted to one another. That attraction was now gone, turned to disdain, even murderous rage.

One night, Isabella found it difficult to sleep. She kept thinking about Howard's infidelity. Her thoughts worked themselves into quiet rage. She got out of bed and walked to the couch where Howard was sleeping. She looked at her husband and thought about how easy it would be to end his life. His face looked so stupid. How many times had he cheated on her?

She could make it look like an accident. He could suffocate in his sleep. He could fall off the couch and hit his head, never to wake up again. Maybe he could overdose on some drug? She would be the poor widow that didn't know her husband was an addict. So many possibilities.

Howard began to stir, and Isabella went back into the bedroom. She wrestled with her thoughts. She was not a murderer. She was appalled at her thoughts and closed her eyes and tried to think of the days that lay ahead.

Howard woke in the morning and decided to get breakfast for his wife. He drove over to Isabella's favorite restaurant and bought her usual meal: eggs, bacon, toasted Cuban bread and, most importantly, a cup of Cuban coffee called a *cortadito*. She loved the sweetness of it, and Howard hoped it would put her into a better mood.

He drove back to the apartment with the breakfast. Isabella was still sleeping so he placed the meal on the kitchen table with a note:

My dearest Isabella:
    Please enjoy your breakfast. I love you and want to take care of you forever.

He knew such a small act could not make up for what he'd done. He left the apartment for the university.

Isabella woke and was greeted by a delicious smell. She

walked to the kitchen and saw the spread. She read the note and it put a smile on her face. She felt incredibly guilty for her horrible thoughts during the night.

Isabella opened the box and began to eat. Somehow, she had to find the courage to forgive her husband, as difficult as it was. Isabella knew Howard loved her and wanted them to be a happy family. After she ate, she sent Howard a text to say thank you.

After the long days of depression in the little apartment, he felt like they were going to make it.

57

CARLOS WAS DRIVING HOME AFTER A LONG AND BORING DAY OF paperwork at the office. Donovan had not given his two-week notice and was considered missing. Chief Vargas forwarded an email asking about him, and Carlos promptly ignored it. It was better not to mention anything and just let sleeping dogs lie. Chief Vargas could fire Carlos for following a suspect into a foreign country.

Carlos drove down US-1 and went to the local shopping mall. He had to buy a new belt, as he lost a significant amount of weight. On his way, he passed the food court and picked up a soda. He heard a popping noise that sounded like a hammer. The noise continued. No one seemed to notice, but Carlos knew it was gunfire. He took a long sip of his soda and threw it to the floor as he ran toward the gunfire. He pulled the fire alarm to get people out of harm's way, but it was too late.

Carlos saw a young white male running in his direction, firing indiscriminately behind him. He got behind a trash can and fired a shot into the young man's knee to stop him from firing. He fell into a heap on the floor, and his gun slid a few feet from Carlos.

Carlos saw three young Latino males, who fired twice. He missed one but got the other in the stomach. Carlos lay flat on the floor and fired three more rounds, hitting the person he missed in the leg, and the third person in the shoulder. Carlos felt like he had the situation under control. He yelled at the three, "Toss your weapons toward me and put your hands behind your back!"

Two of the three individuals did so. The third refused and shouted at his companions, "Shoot his ass."

Carlos' eyes trained on the young man. He was shot in the shoulder and had difficulty positioning the weapon. Carlos got back on the floor and aimed for the uncooperative kid's head. He repeated the order to drop the weapon. Onlookers were now gathering around the spectacle. Carlos spotted a teen, possibly a tourist, licking an ice-cream cone and watching with great delight. It was very surreal for Carlos, but he kept his focus on the aggressor. The teen finally threw his weapon, seeing the futility of it all, and Carlos kept his gun trained on the four until backup arrived.

It took fifteen minutes for the police to show up. The four gunmen were cuffed and then sent to jail. Carlos spoke to the arresting officers, and they congratulated him for a job well done. Carlos was concerned about firing his gun in a public place, but after some encouraging words from arresting officers, felt confident enough that there would be no backlash.

Chief Vargas arrived on the scene after forty minutes.

Carlos was smiling for once.

"Carlos, congratulations. You deserve much praise for this. The evening news crew should be here shortly. This is your moment of glory, so go speak to them. Be short with the details but let them know it was all you. You took care of this all by yourself. It must have taken courage."

"I was scared, I tell you. I dropped my soda and just ran

toward the gunfire. I also pulled a fire alarm, not quite sure if that was the right thing to do."

"Stop being such a modest asshole and enjoy the moment. Not many people would do what you did. I would've thought twice going in without backup like that," said a voice behind Carlos.

It was Wayne. The two partners exchanged hugs.

Carlos was on the evening news that night. He was ecstatic about the whole experience. Carlos, Wayne, Chief Vargas, and the entire department went out for drinks after. Not once did he pull out his wallet, as everyone wanted to buy him a drink. They celebrated long into the night. Carlos felt like a cop again, which was a feeling he had not felt in a very long time. He stopped a major shootout in a public space. It could have ended badly for many people that evening if it were not for his quick thinking.

* * *

Late in the evening, Steve was disembarking the plane returning from Turks and Caicos. He was unhappy, and a huge frown was plastered on his face. As he passed through Customs, he noticed all the smiling faces and goofy braids that donned women's hair. He walked to his car and happened upon a television. The headline read "Local Cop Stops Major Shootout". He saw Carlos and Wayne being interviewed. They were smiling on camera. He also saw footage from the security cameras. Steve overheard a woman next to him talking on the phone. "Did you hear about that shooting? Yeah, that mall ... that cop was amazing. I'd like to meet him. He's hot for an old guy."

Steve began to feel his face burning. His hands became sweaty. He was overwhelmed with emotions he had not experienced since he was a child: envy. He felt like an absolute loser compared to Carlos. His thoughts went from jealousy to hatred. If people only knew the laws that so-called officer broke. That was not a good guy. He was part of the problem. Steve wanted to erase his memory from the planet.

Steve pushed his way out of the crowd that had gathered around the television, got his bags, and exited the terminal. He found his car parked where he left it. He turned on the car's ignition and began to back out. He was lost in his thoughts, thinking about Natasha and Carlos, when suddenly he heard a horn blaring. The sound was deafening, and it shook Steve back into reality.

A young lady behind the wheel began to point and scream at him. In shock, Steve watched the woman gesticulating and after a few seconds, she drove off.

Steve was now enraged to the point that he lost all reason. He threw his car into drive and accelerated. He caught up with her after a few seconds. Steve blew the horn, which made the woman swerve back and forth. She accelerated out of the garage and tried to get on the highway, running two red lights. Steve followed closely, laughing to himself, and blaring the horn as he went. Steve turned off the lights and accelerated, pulling up next to her to get a better look. Steve noticed the woman's face. It was clear to him that she was completely afraid.

He shouted, "Not so tough now, you stupid bimbo!" He got in front of her and slowed down, effectively brake-checking her.

She moved into the next lane abruptly, trying her best to get away from Steve. She overcompensated and began to fish-tail. Steve slowed down, getting behind her to watch the crash unfold. The woman's car swerved back and forth as she tried to regain control. She turned hard left to regain control as she went offroad, resulting in the car rolling over. Steve counted rotations with great delight.

"Woo. Take that! I needed some good news in my life," Steve

cried out as he slowed down and pulled to the side of the road. He felt strong again, knowing that someone got what they deserved. Other people began to pull over. Some were getting out to help. Seeing a crowd forming, Steve came back to his senses. He began to worry that someone might have seen him, and so he calmly got back on the road and drove home.

Steve got home and took a long shower. It was great to be back in familiar surroundings. After an hour, he turned on the local news to see if the accident made the news. The accident was a feature story. The newscaster described the accident. "There was a road rage incident a mile away from Miami International Airport. It is reported that a crazed driver followed an innocent woman, forcing her off the road."

Steve laughed out loud like he was watching a Marx Brothers' movie. "Innocent? Give me a break. They have no idea. She started it first. She got what she deserved!" He quieted himself down to hear eye-witness reports. Fortunately, no one had spotted Steve's license plate; even the security cameras had not picked up the plate. The report continued. "The woman, Natalie Hernandez Rodriquez, died at the scene. She was thirty-five and leaves six children."

"Another one bites the dust. People shouldn't play around with me. I keep telling everyone. Now, they understand. Soon, everyone will know what happens. I'm the real hero. I'm the one that cleans up the streets, not Carlos, and certainly not that cowboy douchebag. That woman was clearly unbalanced. I did the world a favor."

Steve commemorated the occasion by listening to Richard Wagner's "Tannhäuser Overture". He pretended to conduct the orchestra. Alone in his apartment, he celebrated his victories against all those who'd slighted him. He looked at his accomplishments and remembered that he needed to unpack his bag.

He placed his bag on his bed, opened it, tossed dirty clothes in the hamper and folded his clean ones neatly into a drawer.

He put the dreadlocks he'd purchased on his head, laughing to himself, remembering how he stole the Taino knife. Suddenly, Steve stopped laughing. His eyes glazed over, his smile turning into a vile sneer.

Gently, he took out a package from his bag. It was wrapped carefully in tissue paper. He placed the package on the desk, removing the tissue bit by bit until it revealed the pilfered knife. It was not fragile in any way, but Steve wanted to be extremely careful. He cradled the knife in his hands and brought it to his lips saying, "I have important plans for you."

58

STEVE HAD BEEN PLOTTING HIS FINAL REVENGE FOR MONTHS. HE could not wait to watch his archnemesis suffer. For Steve, Jane stood in the way of everything. She did not come from an abusive home and had the love and support of her family, which was something that Steve longed to have.

It was time to make Jane pay. Steve drove to her home at 9 p.m. Jane had just showered and was reading a novel in bed. She had neither purchased security cameras, nor turned on her security alarm. Steve found that the kitchen window was open and he simply climbed in. Silently, he crept down the hall and entered Jane's bedroom with a black ski mask.

"Don't say a word," said Steve. He took off the backpack and sat it on the ground.

Jane threw her book in the air and put her hands in front of her face. "What do you want? Please don't hurt me. I've got jewelry in my closet."

"I don't want your jewelry." Steve took off the mask from his face. "It's great to see you, Jane."

Jane gasped in complete shock. Her suspicions were regretfully confirmed. However, at that moment, she did not quite make the connection between Steve and her possible death.

"Come on! This is too far. I'm going to call the cops!" yelled Jane.

Steve came closer and took out the Taino knife. "No, you won't. I will shoot you and gut you like a fish."

"What do you want from me, Steve? I know it was you who put the alligator in my house."

"And don't forget the raccoons."

"You're a nightmare."

Steve placed the gun to Jane's head and said, "You don't even know the half of it." He started to smile.

"What do you want me to do? Please don't kill me." Jane started to breathe heavily. "I can support your promotion to full professor. I can talk to the dean."

"Oh, thank you! That's so nice of you. Would you, *really*? It's far too late for that now." Steve grabbed a piece of paper and a pen from the desk next to her bed.

"What's this for?"

"This is your last assignment. Are you ready to write?"

"Is this a contract about my willingness to support your tenure?"

"You don't realize what's going on? We're way beyond all that, Jane. This is the end." Steve put the gun to her head with one hand and shoved the paper in her face with the other. "And this is your suicide note."

"Come on," said Jane. "Please don't do this. I will do whatever you want."

Steve wanted her to sign a letter that he wrote, saying that she hated what she had become and could not deal with the stress of killing Natasha and Victoria Lane, the divorce attorney. Victoria Lane represented Jane's husband when he filed for divorce. The letter said that Victoria ruined Jane's life.

Jane could not stop crying.

"I'm not going to sign the letter. I refuse! You won't get away with this, Steve. Someone will get to the bottom of this and figure out it was you."

"I'm invisible, Jane. I also wanted to let you know that I have had a little pen pal. His name is Carlos Garcia. The killer— *you're* the killer, in case you forgot—wrote him two letters confessing to the crimes."

"You're evil."

Steve pulled out a rope from his backpack.

"Your time has come, my dear associate dean."

"Please. Don't do this, Steve. You will regret this."

"Regret this? No, I've been waiting to do this for a very long time. You've been a thorn in my side for years," responded Steve nonchalantly.

"I don't want to die."

"Someone has to pay for my crimes, Jane. It's the only way I can get away with them. It might as well be you. I killed Natasha and many others, but I'm not going down for this. The letter you just wrote to Detective Garcia explains your rage against Natasha." Steve started to laugh. "I wrote that you were in a romantic relationship with a student, and Natasha threatened to report you to Human Resources. She wanted to get an A in your class, and you made her life a living nightmare. She got her first B in your course and became obsessed with getting revenge. You had to stop her before she ruined your career."

"I hate you. I wish that I'd never met you. You are the worst thing that has ever happened to me," screamed Jane hysterically.

"Tough words. That doesn't sound very professional or associate dean-like. You always were a robot: all business with no consideration for other people's feelings, hard work, and effort." Steve shrugged. "It gets better. I also posted a fake paper written by you where you plagiarize an article that Natasha wrote. This is all written in the letter. I tell you, Jane, I've never worked so hard on an academic paper. Writing about tax fraud sure is boring."

"Please. I beg you."

"Beg me? Beg me? Ha! Put the rope around your neck," ordered Steve.

Jane hesitated.

"Too late." Steve approached Jane with the gun in his hand. "Now, sign the letter."

"Never!"

"Sign it," screamed Steve.

"Rot in hell."

Steve grabbed Jane's hand and forced her to sign the letter. She resisted but he overpowered her. He wore rubber gloves to avoid leaving DNA traces. Steve became more enraged and after some time convinced Jane to kill herself. Steve spent another hour cleaning up the crime scene. He made sure that there were no loose ends to his scheme.

Then he drove back to his apartment in Brickell. He was smiling from ear to ear. The deed was finally done. Jane would go down in history as an evil law professor known for three brutal murders of innocent people. The public would wonder how such a talented law professor could have committed such senseless and brutal crimes. They would question how she slipped through the cracks of the hiring committees. The public would ask why nobody noticed that she was a psychopath. Friends, colleagues, and neighbors will start to question who among them is a serial killer.

Thanks to his masterful work, nobody would ever trust their professor again.

59

CARLOS PORED OVER THE KILLER'S LETTERS FOR DAYS. THE KILLER confessed to the crimes and said that Natasha was dead. The killer said that Natasha was "swimming with the fish in the ocean". The letters contained several photos of Natasha's dead body.

At times, Carlos could not control his emotions. There were several occasions at the office where he threw papers across the floor. He screamed, and then started to cry. Chief Vargas told Carlos that she was going to take him off the case. She said that it was too personal for him, and he was losing his objectivity.

"I should have never let you stay on the case," said Chief Vargas. "Officers should never work crimes involving their immediate family."

"I've been nothing but professional, Chief Vargas. Please let me see this case through to the end."

"I will. But I want daily reports from Wayne. If I see you burst into tears or throw one more thing, I'm taking you off the case. This is not good for your emotional health. We need you. You're one of the best detectives we have. I don't want to see you washed up in six months," Chief Vargas stated solemnly.

Carlos and Wayne showed up at Jane's home. They found her suicide note. They spent an hour going over the crime scene.

"I got the criminal profile all wrong. I always suspected it was Steve, but we didn't have any proof," said Carlos.

"Sometimes, it's the ones that you least expect. Who would have thought that this Ivy League-educated associate dean was a monster?" asked Wayne.

"It just doesn't make any sense," responded Carlos.

"The world is screwed up," said Wayne and took a deep breath.

Carlos had a gut feeling that something was fishy, but he did not have any evidence. He kept saying, "It just doesn't add up."

"Be happy we closed the case," said Wayne. "Justice is served. We did our jobs. A victory for the Miami Dade Police."

60

It was a sunny day, and Steve was in a great mood. The newspapers had a field day with stories of the killer associate dean. There were dozens of stories in every major newspaper across the world. A few journalists had already shopped around book proposals to editors at various publishing houses.

Steve sat in his kitchen and enjoyed reading the stories about Jane. He could not stop smiling. He decided to go for a run around Brickell. He felt like he could run five marathons. His arch-nemesis was gone, and her reputation was ruined forever. Nobody would ever remember Jane for her scholarly accomplishments. Her great teaching evaluations would never be brought up by other faculty at the law school. Jane would only be remembered as a brutal serial killer.

The law school faculty was stunned; the members never thought that she would be capable of such heinous crimes. The public-relations team at the university went into crisis management mode. The leadership at the university did not sleep more than five hours during the first week, as they addressed this horrific story.

All these things motivated Steve as he ran along the water.

He came back after an hour run. He said hello to the doorman at his building. "Life is great. Isn't it?"

"Yes, sir. Have a great day," said the doorman. Weird, the doorman thought. That guy had never talked to him, and he'd worked there for ten years.

Steve took his boat out to the Everglades to celebrate. Like many serial killers, he revisited the grave sites of his victims. He felt chills go down his spine as he approached the spot where he'd dumped Natasha's body.

Steve watched several alligators swim toward him in the distance. Steve took out a bottle of water from his cooler and raised the bottle into the air. "To my favorite associate dean."

AUTHORS' NOTE

This novel is fiction. No characters are based on any real people.

ACKNOWLEDGMENTS

Thanks to the amazing team at Next Chapter for their hard work and dedication. It was such a pleasure to work with this talented group of individuals. We also would like to give a special thanks to Shannon Evans for her editorial assistance.

ABOUT THE AUTHORS

Jonathan D. Rosen lives in New Jersey. He has published two novels and twenty non-fiction books.

To learn more about Jonathan D. Rosen and discover more Next Chapter authors, visit our website at www.nextchapter.pub.

* * *

Amin Nasser lives in North Carolina. He has published nineteen non-fiction books.

Professor Law
ISBN: 978-4-82415-424-8

Published by
Next Chapter
2-5-6 SANNO
SANNO BRIDGE
143-0023 Ota-Ku, Tokyo
+818035793528

19th October 2022

Lightning Source UK Ltd.
Milton Keynes UK
UKHW010100100223
416720UK00001B/234